DAEMON'S BLOOD

ATIERNAN BOOK ONE: DAEMON BLADE SERIES

LANA SKY

Daemon's Blood

Daemon's Blood By Lana Sky

———————)•••••

Cover Design and Interior Formatting by Charity Chimni
Editing by Charity Chimni

ACKNOWLEDGMENTS

Thanks so much to everyone who supported this draft along the way, including the many beta readers who provided encouragement! Please keep in mind that this story includes dark, graphic, and explicit content matter that may not be suitable for readers under the age of 18—or for readers who are uncomfortable with the following subject matter: age-gap relationships, explicit sex, and graphic depictions of violence.

CHAPTER
ONE

P ride always came before a fall—but that was only half of the tale. *Trust* came first. As a witch, Miranda wasn't well versed in all mortal legends, but she knew the gist of some. Like the one about the figure they considered to be the evilest of all, well into the twenty-first century.

Lucifer.

According to the most popular account, he had been an angel initially, and none had foreseen his downfall until the very day he assaulted heaven as the devil himself. Unbeknownst to the mortals, the truth was far more nuanced.

The warrior known as Lucifer had been a daemon lord beloved by those in his orbit. Scores of mortals and immortals alike had blindly put their faith in his leadership. Most refused to acknowledge the darkness growing within him until it was too late. All suffered in the end.

That was the irony of it—when someone fell from grace, they tended to take *everyone* down with them—and the gravest consequences usually affected those who had no say in the original sin.

For such souls, pride was the last resort. One last shred of dignity to cling to. Shunned by her own coven, Miranda wholeheartedly credited her survival until this point to nothing but pride.

Therefore, she had no qualms about holding her head high and facing this newest obstacle with her chin in the air. Already, she had sunk about as far as you could go—literally. Trapped in a daemon's dungeon, abducted from her homeland, and stripped of her magic...

How much worse could it get?

Exponentially worse, a part of her warned as a sudden noise shattered the quiet. Footsteps? There wasn't even time to compose herself as the door to her cell flew open. Blinking, she strained her eyes through the impenetrable darkness for a glimpse of the intruder. One of *them*, come to gawk at the captive witch?

Surprisingly, this figure would be the first to face her. Despite being inherently violent, these daemons didn't seem inclined to gloat. After days in near-total darkness, the only other living creatures she'd seen were the rats scurrying in the corners of the cell.

Miranda assumed this visitor was the same unseen figure who brought her food every day, slipping a tray through a gap in the door. The same person gruffly revealed her fate when she awoke here two days ago.

But no...

The door opened fully, revealing a massive silhouette with piercing amber eyes bright enough to rival the shadows. She swallowed hard. Only a sparse knowledge of daemon history allowed her to place him. Few men, mortal or otherwise, had eyes like his, a reddish orange like hellfire. But would he really deign to visit the dungeon to gawk at his captive? A creature who spawned legends with blood and death...

The fearsome Blood Warrior.

"Witch." His voice was so deep, something inside her quivered at the sound. The low baritone alone convinced her fully. It was *him*.

So, the daemon lord hadn't stooped to sending a minion to fetch her.

He had come for her himself.

"Do you know where you are now?" he asked. The probing nature of that question unnerved her.

Of course, she knew. One minute she'd been picking herbs in the gardens just beyond the boundaries of her coven. The next...

Darkness. From the way her head had throbbed when she first regained consciousness, she guessed she'd fallen prey to a potent, very crude sleeping spell. One that rendered her unconscious long enough to allow her to be transferred here without a fight—somewhere within the daemon realm, most likely.

A rather anti-climactic kidnapping.

Not long after, when she'd barely realized her current circumstances, a tray had appeared from under the door, and a voice had whispered, "You are in the dungeon of Lord…"

Something.

It was so strange that she couldn't remember his name. All she knew were the legends starring him, and that he was called something foreign and ancient sounding. Evil. Introductions aside, he didn't seem inclined to use *her* name either.

"Get up," he rasped, displaying a fluent grasp of a mortal language.

Miranda lurched to her feet and staggered to find her balance. She had mentally rehearsed this moment every second of her imprisonment. Practiced how she would throw her head back and laugh when the monster made his demands. Be brave.

But, partially illuminated by the glow of a nearby torch, he looked…

Feral. Every inch of him seemed to convey strength and vitality. He even smelled powerful, with a scent that itched at her nostrils like wood smoke. His hair was red, like blood, and so long it draped his shoulders like a cape—

though the alarming hue didn't make the length seem feminine. Instead, it just highlighted the amber in his eyes, raising goosebumps along her skin.

He looked nothing like the religious iterations of daemons most mortals feared. Ironically, he resembled a textbook example of a vampire—though, his breed was what the legends were based on, after all.

Raeth daemons. Creatures born of Hell itself, who fed on blood and dwelled in shadow, hunting mortals and witches alike for sport. The worst among them utilized the most despised and archaic of all arcane practices—blood magic.

No wonder her kind feared the likes of him. Though…up until now, Miranda would have proudly scoffed at the thought of ever being cowed by a man, immortal or not. Faced with him in person, she quietly reassessed her entire strategy.

It didn't help that he remained silent, observing her as intently as she did him. As his eyes raked over her body a second time, she self-consciously wrestled the hem of her filthy dress down to her knees. She couldn't imagine how she might have looked. There wasn't a bathroom in this cell —only a bucket she'd been forced to use when the bodily urge arose. There wasn't even a mirror or rag she could utilize to keep herself clean, not that she cared to make herself presentable for a daemon. She hoped her body odor and haggard appearance offended him.

Though, what he actually thought? She had no idea—his expression was stone.

That didn't stop her mind from conjuring plenty of despicable acts he might look to commit next. Would he hurt her? Rip her to pieces? Or, the most horrific crime of all, drain her blood?

"Come." Without so much as a threat or curse, he inclined his head for her to follow, and she was left stunned.

On trembling legs, she tip-toed after him into a wide corridor and instantly felt as though she stepped back in time. Her coven was openly mocked as a more "old-fashioned" bunch, but even they included some modern elements into their lives, such as cell phones and cars. The internet occasionally had its uses, and Miranda herself owned an automatic coffee maker, which had served to ostracize her no more than she already was.

Seeing as how torchlight served as the sole illumination, she doubted this place had access to electricity. Even so, her eyes were watering at the harsh light after days in shadow.

But at least it hadn't been total darkness, a part of her admitted. The light visible beneath the solid door of her cell had barely been enough to see her hand in front of her face, and yet it alone had made this imprisonment bearable. *You got through that without breaking; you can survive anything.*

Except for a short walk, it seemed. The dungeon stretched endlessly, weaving through darkness and shadow and imposing black stone. She lost track of how long they wandered.

It felt like an eternity—perhaps because her silent guide didn't speak. Massive and slow moving, he just led the way toward a set of stairs that seemed cut into the building's foundation. Suddenly, his voice rumbled back to her.

"Watch your step."

The warning—right as she stumbled over a steep step cut into the stone anyway—startled Miranda so badly she gasped. Before she could puzzle out why he would warn her at all, the daemon had already mounted the staircase and disappeared through a doorway.

With thoughts of her rodent roommates at the back of her mind, she scrambled after him, already panting by the time she rounded a corner and entered a massive room, so brightly lit it had her blinking.

There went the no electricity theory—ornate light fixtures sported bulbs that were brilliantly illuminated. The place was grand—she had to give him that much. Dark and gothic, it reminded her of a castle, complete with smooth stone floors.

She could sense, rather than see, other creatures lurking beyond view, but she didn't dare turn her gaze from the warrior's back to get a good look. While most daemons lived alone, she remembered from her studies, that some preferred to stay in colonies, with whole families living together under one roof.

Ironically, in Hazel's Way, her own coven lived similarly—though this dwelling was far more lavish than any in their sacred forest. This level was a stark contrast to the dungeon, beautifully furnished with plush red carpet covering polished flagstones.

"Witch."

Belatedly, she realized that she had stopped to gape. Her daemon guide was halfway across the expansive room, eyeing her from over his shoulder with a look that made her swallow.

"Come." Sternly, he inclined his head, and Miranda had no choice but to follow.

This walk wasn't as grueling, at least. Near the end of the hall, he turned into another spacious room that resembled a training area with weapons—everything spanning from swords to daggers—displayed on metal racks and open space in the center, dominated by just two other figures.

Instantly, Miranda realized that daemons had a very different concept of hospitality than witches. In Hazel's Way, guests were presented with warm tea and cheerful greetings.

Not dead monsters ripped right from a nightmare.

She recoiled in disgust, covering her nose with her hand as a putrid stench rankled her nostrils.

She had studied a variety of beasts while scouring old magical texts, and even the odd mortal movie or two. Nothing compared to whatever this monster was, glaring up at her from a bloodstained section of stone.

"Keep back," the warrior warned, though she wasn't inclined to disobey. "Its blood is acidic and will burn your skin."

Poisonous qualities aside, the thing was also massive—twice the size of the biggest man she knew. Its limbs were surprisingly humanlike, attached to a stocky torso. Gray skin revealed hints of the blackish veins snaking beneath, while a pelt of coarse brown hair obscured its privates and vast skull. Its face, however, was grotesque with red eyes and a mouth full of sharp fangs.

"My Lord, we retrieved the body of this beast as you requested." Another daemon male stood over the creature, dressed head to toe in black. If she didn't know better, she'd think he were handsome, with long, dark hair pulled back from a delicate face.

As it was, he was an evil, corrupted creature that only superficially resembled mortals, no different than the beast he inspected. So focused on his observation, he addressed his master without looking up. When he finally did, and spotted Miranda in the doorway, his expression went cold. The disgust was mutual, it seemed. "You bring her here? Lord Atiernan, she is—"

"She can't do you any harm, Benjamin," the red-haired daemon said, nodding to her wrist.

Oh. Miranda flinched and eyed the metal bracelet in question. It was beautiful at a glance, made of silver, etched with various swirling designs. Something far too extravagant to award a captive.

At least, on the surface. To no avail, Miranda had spent every second of her captivity in the dungeon trying to pry it off. It was a binding circle, intended to suppress her power completely. While wearing it, she was helpless.

"Witch," the red-haired lord continued, drawing her attention to him. "Look—" he gestured toward the slain creature, but his expression wasn't full of malice like one would expect. This display wasn't meant to intimidate her. But then, what? "Tell me what you see."

"A monster," she rasped, wringing her hands together to hide how they trembled.

"No."

Miranda jumped—she must have walked a few steps ahead of him, because his hot breath tickled the back of her neck though she didn't dare turn to see how close he might be. Was that a laugh that rumbled from his throat next? Or a growl.

"Tell me if there is anything odd you find about this creature. Look carefully."

A test? She could refuse, but some faint, internal voice warned that this man didn't tolerate defiance from anyone.

For that reason, she'd hesitated to take him in fully until now. When she finally did, she was disappointed to find that the shadows of the dungeon weren't solely responsible for making him appear so intimidating. With a face as ruthlessly handsome as if carved from stone, and that mane of scarlet hair, he resembled a god, bathed in the sunlight streaming in from a row of tall windows behind him.

Witches honored several gods—all women, symbolizing femininity, wisdom, and nurturing. Masculine, physical strength was a trait valued in other cultures. He would suit some obscure figure the ancient humans might have worshiped. A paragon of bloodshed and war.

Ironically, rather than chainmail or armor, a simple black shirt and slacks clothed his muscular frame. The plain ensemble didn't diminish him any. He looked liable to grab one of the nearby swords and wield it against any enemy—her included.

"Look," he commanded, his voice booming. "I will not ask again."

She recognized that tone—next time, he would punish her disobedience outright. Did daemon torture differ much from what she was used to?

More than likely, yes.

Swallowing her disgust, Miranda inched closer to the slain beast. On second glance, she saw exactly what the daemon referred to—a black mark marring the pale flesh on the monster's chest. It looked like dirt at first, but as she crouched down, skirting a gleaming puddle of black blood, she saw that it wasn't natural. Suddenly, the beast's human-like proportions took on a sinister insinuation.

Before she could stop herself, she voiced her suspicions out loud. "This creature was made by magic. Or warped by it. With a spell…"

Not any spell, she realized, horrified. The marking was a specific type of rune used only by a handful of covens—hers included. While crude in execution, its use was simple to understand—any beast sporting this mark would be frenzied, liable to attack its quarry with vicious ferocity.

But that confounded her further. Why would a witch from Hazel's Way be bold enough to send a hoard of crazed monsters after a pack of daemons?

Though, hell, she almost wished she'd thought of the idea herself.

"We call the beast a sentinel," the man, Atiernan, explained while advancing with heavy footsteps. "Tell me, witch. What kind of spell could create such a creature?"

"I…" Miranda cleared her throat—after days of silence, her voice rasped, hoarse and weak. "One intended to send it here, perhaps." She couldn't resist shuffling even closer, just enough to finger part of the brand. It felt crusty, as if burned there by a hot object. Or very twisted magic. "Perhaps to control it."

"There were other sentinels with this mark," the lord explained. "Hordes that attack by the day. They kill ruthlessly, and can take down three men apiece before being killed. Can you counteract this spell?"

"It would take effort," Miranda said absently. Tracking magic was a skill well beyond her wheelhouse. Still, with time and proper resources, anything was possible—her entire life had been lived by that mantra. And suddenly… she knew why she wasn't dead.

"No." Her voice shook, eyes narrowing as she spun to face the daemon lord. "I won't help you."

Even the possibility felt like some cruel test designed by her mother to reinforce the vicious truth Miranda had been fed her whole life—*You are a monster who belongs in Hell among your kind...*

"You have been kept safe and unharmed," Atiernan pointed out, drawing her attention back to him. "Help me, and you will be returned to your coven—"

"No! You might as well kill me now," she added in a whisper as those sharp amber eyes pierced her to the very core. Still, she raised her voice, emphasizing every word. Her mother, or anyone else who doubted her heritage as a witch could choke on each one. "I will never help a daemon. You all. Deserve. To *die*."

CHAPTER
TWO

I f Atiernan had learned anything after more than a few thousand years of life, it was that the relationships mortals formed were weak, easily shattered by infidelity or petty arguments.

Daemons couldn't afford such a luxury. In the end, allies could be all that separated a man from a nasty death. It didn't matter if those companions had betrayed you in the past—fuck, you didn't even have to *like* them.

But you honored your own and watched their back when the time came to do so.

By that philosophy, retribution was handled much in the same way. If one member of a family—or a coven of witches, for example—committed an unspeakable atrocity, then only someone from said clan could right the wrong. Whether they wanted to or not, no matter how much time may have passed. For that reason alone, he had kidnapped a witch from the mortal realm. To be fair, he merely intended to ask for her help.

Though he should have every right to torture her for assistance if he had to.

After all, one of her kind dared to attack him and his people first. Though, Atiernan would be lying if he claimed that was the sole reason behind his disdain for the race. Thousands of years in the making, his feud with the coven of Hazel had been a long time coming.

At least the drama kept things lively. Life in his territory—without the glory of war or bloodshed—had grown dull over the last few centuries. Imprisoning a witch was the sort of thing needed to snap him from the rut.

Or, make him reconsider his equally long abstinence from blood.

Damn her. Coldly, Atiernan eyed the woman in question, taking in her short, thin frame, brown hair, and equally dark eyes. From her plain brown dress, she wasn't high ranking in her little coven. Perhaps someone on the lowest rung, though she held his gaze unflinchingly.

He wasn't fooled—her strength was a façade meant to disguise how she trembled. Before her capture, he had only learned enough about her to decide that she made a fitting candidate for what he had in mind—Miranda Lightwood, a powerful, though isolated witch on the outskirts of her coven. In person, she held none of the charm he would have suspected from someone so shunned by the others. She was nothing like...

"I won't help you," the witch hissed, her voice surprisingly steady. Especially when he could hear her fluttering pulse halfway across the room. Regardless, she earned a grudging kernel of his respect.

He saw the recognition in her eyes—a familiarity of him based on faulty witch knowledge that portrayed him and his kind to be monsters and killers. A rather convenient description when the witches' long history of oppression toward daemons was considered. Lies aside, she knew what he was capable of. All he had to do was snap her neck. Drain her dry. Torture her. All things he would have been more than happy to do not long ago.

Something about her unsettled him. She wasn't beautiful. No, she was small, haughty, and had her nose shoved so damn high in the air it was a wonder she could still walk and maintain her balance. In his days as a warrior, wooing whichever woman he fancied, he would have passed her over without a second glance. If it weren't for her scent…

Amid the death and decay in the room was a softer aroma that did something to him no mortal or daemon in the past few hundred years had been able to do. It stopped him cold and made him do a double take. The crisp smell flooded his nostrils, making his throat go dry with every new intake. Alone with her in the closeness of the dungeon, it had been a struggle to leave her untouched. To keep from sneaking a small little taste of her blood. Just a sip.

It had been so long since he'd tasted a witch…

Or anyone.

Sure, his kind kept willing humans in the manor to feed upon, but none of them enticed Atiernan quite so much. Maybe it was because...he *knew* she would resist? She would fight like hell, making the moment she finally surrendered, and she *would* surrender, all the sweeter...

"You might as well kill me now," the woman in question croaked, her eyes narrowed to slits. "Hear me well, daemon —I will never help you or your kind. Never."

It was a good thing, then, that she was merely a backup plan. After arranging for her capture, it had taken him two days to track and dispatch a sentinel alone—at no small risk to himself, either. This was their one shot at finding answers behind the creatures' sudden appearance.

One way or another.

"Are you ready, sir?" Benjamin, his second in command, asked from his position near the dead sentinel.

Given their shared history with witches, Ben didn't look at all pleased by the presence of one. An opponent of his plan from the very start, Atiernan had shared hardly any details with his most loyal soldier. While he trusted the daemon with his life, hate was a powerful emotion few could overcome—and his people had several damn good reasons to mistrust that magical race. Even the mortals had a saying among themselves that he figured was fitting in this instance —better to ask forgiveness than permission.

"I'm ready." With a nod, Atiernan sank into a crouch near the creature's massive skull. Extending two fingers, he prodded the sentinel's eye sockets, heedless of the ruby irises glaring up at him, frozen in death. With no hesitation, he dug his nails into the flesh and closed his eyes—ignoring the sting of its blood eating away at his flesh. Unlike the witch, he could heal from the damage easily. Once his mind was sufficiently calm, he dove his consciousness into the remnants of the monster's.

Hours since its death, and already its brain was decaying, rendering its recollections fragmented beyond recognition. In the end, he only gleaned one clear image, the last the creature ever saw, apart from him.

Atiernan inspected it ruthlessly, growing more concerned with every new detail. This figure wasn't a witch. No, mere seconds before his arrival, the sentinel had stared down a man with dark eyes, brandishing a blade. The male wasn't from his fortress, either. He wore modern clothing, but his face wasn't one Atiernan recognized. Was he the source of this scourge?

There was no way of knowing for sure.

And, suddenly, this witch was no longer a backup, but his sole hope.

Damn. With a sigh, Atiernan retreated into his own mind and allowed himself a second to adjust. Scrying was a skill few of his kind learned to master. Despite years of honing the craft, he still loathed the concept of crawling through another's thoughts and feelings—be them monster or otherwise.

In fact, today was the first time he'd used the power in decades, only to wind up with an even bigger mystery than before. When he finally opened his eyes, the first sight to greet him was the witch cowering nearby, a fitting punishment.

With her presence alone, the woman mocked him.

"This creature is a corruption twisted by dark magic," he told her, though he knew from her frown that she didn't understand. Or care. "They come from the north in droves, attacking my people indiscriminately. I think the culprit might be a mage. Dark eyes. Black hair. Do you know him?"

She flinched. "You think it was one of us who sent these creatures after you? Then why bring me here? To mock me?" Her cheeks reddened but not with the abject horror one might expect to see in a captive woman. This one seemed utterly disgusted—by him and the mere thought of being useful to a daemon. "I am a witch," she snarled.

"I know what you are," Atiernan replied.

Once again, she didn't react the way he'd anticipated—with a prideful snarl. She shivered, and her eyes went so wide he could see his reflection. Apparently, witches these days didn't prefer to be called so to their faces.

"In any case, you recognize this magic?" he prodded.

She startled at the question, and renewed hatred flashed in her gaze. "Of course, I do, not that I'll lift a damn finger to help you counteract it. In fact, I hope those monsters rip you all to pieces!"

And that was Atiernan's cue to go.

Without a second glance at the woman, he stood and left the room, leaving Benjamin to deal with her.

He'd barely reentered the great hall when a figure peeled from the wall to saunter in his direction. "I'm glad to see you are in one piece, my lord," came a husky murmur that made him grit his teeth in recognition. *Not now.*

Oblivious to his irritation, the woman continued to approach, tilting her head to view him better. "I've heard that witches are dangerous, deceptive creatures."

They weren't the only race who could claim as much. The woman before him, though entirely mortal, was no less cunning than the witch he'd stolen, just in a very different way. Wearing a tight-fitting ruby dress, and with her dark hair piled on top of her head, she appealed to an instinct far beyond bloodlust.

"Sanna," he said gruffly. "I don't remember requesting your skills in this matter."

Though he could tell she'd been busy serving her purpose to someone—her wrist bled freely, though the scent was faint, like cheap perfume, easy to overlook.

"I know." She smiled, her green eyes sparkling. "I was merely curious, my lord. I wanted to see for myself the woman for whom you risk us all. Though, if her mortal nature has appealed to you, my lord, I wanted to make myself available should you decide to feed."

Her tone was sweet enough to conceal the subtle insult, but Atiernan wasn't fooled. Unfortunately, she had a point.

He risked everyone's safety on his wayward witch. One way or another, he would make this gamble pay off. It had to.

"Have you decided to scry her, my lord? If you did, the wealth of information we might glean could be—"

"Enough." He dismissed Sanna with a wave of his hand. "Back to your duties."

"Yes, my lord." The woman slunk off, her hips swaying with every step, but Atiernan had no trouble turning away.

Her words, however, weren't so easy to overlook. He wanted to ignore her suggestion entirely, though…

A part of him couldn't help but wonder if he should scry the witch and be done with it. Doing so to another living creature without permission was taboo—not to mention liable to wreck the victim's mind. After meeting the witch himself, he was tempted to make an exception. Just how would she look when she finally broke?

Because, against power as vast as his, they *always* broke in the end.

THREE

"Lord Atiernan!"

"What is it?" The warrior snapped while lifting his gaze from the stack of documents that cluttered his desk. It was an aspect of his title most didn't acknowledge. The business side. In between fending off monsters and witches alike, buildings needed to be repaired, bills paid, and people fed.

It was the *business* side of running his pack that kept him up at night, worrying about the safety of the numerous families who put their trust in him. Territories cost money to maintain. Money that had to come from *somewhere…*

It was his job to find out where, while keeping everyone alive in the meantime.

The increasing sentinel attacks complicated things at an unsustainable rate. Soon, the creatures would have them boxed in with no way out of the fortress—a virtual siege.

But that wasn't Beth's fault, he admitted as he noticed the girl shivering in the doorway.

"Lord Atiernan?" Her brown eyes were wider than saucers. Any moment, she seemed likely to faint if he didn't change his tone. The fledgling was usually so shy and docile—it must have taken a major event to bring her to him alone.

"Yes?" He coaxed the girl into his den with a wave of his hand. "What is it?"

Beth took a steadying breath. At a glance, one might think she was a human teenager—not part daemon. Another glance would reveal the two sharp fangs protruding beneath her pink lips. Funny enough, Beth didn't seem to realize the physical change—having a human witch in the house had brought everyone's primal instincts to the surface.

Even *his*. Unlike Beth, he'd mingled with witches before— one in particular who nearly cost him everything. *Her* aroma had been alluring in its own way, light and crisp, but that Miranda…

Her smell was different.

Sharp, it snagged his nose like a fishhook with honeyed undertones that snaked through his veins, rousing a hunger he couldn't deny. Beneath it all was a faint hint of rosebuds that damn near set his body on fire—and yet, the spicy magic in her blood irritated his nostrils so badly he thought he might sneeze.

Good gods above, he had *never* smelled something quite so enticing and yet repulsive.

Even being in the same room as her made his fangs ache. If she smelled so damn good, what would she *taste* like? He licked his lips just thinking of it…

Not that he would ever find out.

With a forced sigh, he returned his attention to Beth. In such a short time, blood had already seeped from her lower lip to dribble down her chin.

"Is something wrong?" she asked fearfully.

He sighed again. The poor girl hadn't developed enough control of her bloodlust to realize that her body was displaying signs of hunger—which only warned him that Miranda needed to go.

Soon. He'd already gotten from her what very little he expected to gain—confirmation that witch magic was behind the sudden surge in sentinel attacks. With or without her help, he would track down the culprit, and they alone would face his wrath.

"Sir," Beth prodded, wringing her hands together over the skirt of her modest gray dress. "I…"

"What is it? Did someone break another fence post?"

He couldn't suppress the anger in his tone. The heightened fear had everyone on edge. The juveniles had taken to fashioning their own weapons out of the compound's territory markers. Woodless, silver-less fence posts were damn expensive.

"No," Beth said with a nervous giggle, and Atiernan couldn't help but wonder if she were one of the culprits. "My mother wants you to come right away. She says it's important, something about the witch—"

Atiernan cut her off with a groan. *Her again.* Miranda. Despite her little show of bravery, he fully intended to return her to her coven unharmed. Though, there was a time he would have done far worse to her first in the name of survival—scrying her for the answers he sought being the least among the list.

After all, he owed that race no loyalty. The last witch he knew had all but destroyed him. Maybe stubborn pride was what held him back now? No longer would Liva and her betrayal have any hold over him. Miranda could thank her gods for his restraint.

Pushing thoughts of her aside, he stood and gestured for Beth to lead the way. "Show me."

Peony wasn't far—huddled within the storeroom she commandeered to practice her magic and potions in. Atiernan groaned through his teeth as he inspected her wiry frame. He wasn't the only one stressed over the sentinels. The woman's long black hair was a ragged mess, and her crooked glasses were fogged by the steam wafting from a portable cauldron in the middle of the room.

At a glance, she almost passed for a witch. If he squinted. Though, no one could take away from the daemon what she'd managed to accomplish in the realm of magic. With only sheer determination, Peony had worked her way to becoming as close to a witch as someone of their kind could.

For that reason and more, she had his respect—though he knew she'd scoff if he admitted as much out loud. After a few millennia by his side, she saw him more like a son than a leader, and she knew him better than anyone—and he knew her. More than enough to realize the makeshift witch was pushing herself too hard.

Her shoulders trembled beneath the thick tunic she wore, her fingers shaking as she rummaged across a narrow table, pinching piles of herbs at random before tossing them into the steaming cauldron.

Atiernan had seen the woman this ragged once before in his life, and that was on the eve of the war that killed her actual son and nearly cost him his soul.

"You know," he began, moving to stand behind her. "I don't think how quickly you work affects the potion itself."

"Oh bah!" Peony shot him a scathing glance from over her shoulder. "What do you know? Speed is everything," she muttered, turning back to her table laden with scattered herbs and vials of muck.

Her hand wavered between a small bottle of black liquid and a pile of twisted leaves. In the end, she added both ingredients to mixture frothing in the cauldron.

"It's all about the *timing*, Atiernan," she scolded from above a fresh cloud of purplish smoke. "Timing, timing, timing—"

A ragged cough tore through her chest, making her reach for the edge of the table. Atiernan frowned, slipping an arm around the woman as she doubled over, alternating between fits of coughing and sneezing.

"She's been like this all day," Beth accused from the doorway. "Killing herself to find answers to the sentinels. All because that damn witch won't help us!"

"Bethaem." Even as she sputtered, Peony's tone was like a whip. "Don't you dare talk like that!"

Atiernan saw Beth roll her eyes, but she had enough sense to do so while her mother's back was still turned. "Yes, mother," she intoned. "But do you really want *her* help? That evil, *selfish* bitch—"

"Bethaem!"

The girl went silent, but not before Atiernan saw fresh blood dribble down her chin. Once again, she'd cut herself on her own fangs, and didn't seem to realize it.

"I didn't raise you to be so crass, girl," Peony went on scathingly. "*'Evil bitch'* or not—*do you know* what that woman could teach us, if she wanted? All the old spells, the old magic! Marvelous things…"

"As if that bit—*witch* would ever teach *us* anything." Beth's shoulders trembled with rage as her voice rose in pitch. "I heard her say so herself. She's going to let us all die."

Atiernan sighed and named their unspoken nemesis. "Miranda."

"Yes!" Both women whirled on him.

"That's right, *Miranda*," Beth scoffed. "Mother wants us to ask her for help—*Her!* As if she hasn't—"

"Oh hush," Peony snarled. "I should box your ears for over-hearing conversations you were not privy to. Besides, you're too young to understand, but *you* must—" Atiernan couldn't help but flinch as she swiveled to face him. "Surely you must realize what an advantage we would have if the witch would only share her magic with us! We could—"

He held up a hand to cut the woman off. "That's where you're wrong, Peony," he said as gently as he could. "If she *would* share her magic with us, I agree, the benefits would be great. But she won't. I think bringing her here at all was a mistake."

The little wench would sooner set them all ablaze with her hated magic rather than help them. Though, if anyone knew how vindictive witches could be, Peony did. Perhaps her gaze had become a little clouded from behind those foggy glasses? All it took was remembering the way Miranda had threatened to use her magic against him for all traces of goodwill toward her kind to vanish.

"Miranda has sworn to all but kill me if I return her powers," he added. "She would never consent to help us. Besides—" A dry smile shaped his lips, though the topic wasn't the least bit amusing. "Could you imagine what would happen if I allowed her to go free?"

Beth shuddered at the hypothetical situation. Peony, on the other hand, appeared unimpressed.

"How can you be so sure?" she countered. "Have you even asked the woman? Without threats or coercion, or anger? Just *asked* her like a civilized creature, and not some brute? I'm convinced the sentinels are being controlled by magic. Break the spell—we end their reign of terror. Surely you realize that?"

Atiernan shrugged. Obviously, Peony had never been alone with the woman.

"This conversation is over," he said forcefully, turning on his heel. "I'm sending her back—"

"Oh no, you don't, Atiernan," Peony snapped. If he wasn't mistaken, this was the same tone she used to keep Beth in line. "Look at me."

A growl ripped from his throat, but it was primarily for show. He had no choice but to turn like a whipped child.

"What is more important to you," Peony began, hands on her hips, "*your* pride, or the lives of those in your pack? Scores of our people who put their faith in you alone?"

It was a question not even worth a reply. Still, Atiernan did anyway. "You know the answer to that. All of you mean more to me than anything."

"Good," Peony said tightly with a nod of her chin. "Then you know what you need to do. Soon. I know your history with witches, but that is in the past. Our future is all that matters now. Agreed?"

"Atiernan!" Beth balled her hands into fists, unaware of the fact that her tiny fangs were still boring holes through her bottom lip. "You can't! Y-you can't go to her—we don't need *her* help!"

That was where Beth was wrong. Even Atiernan could admit it. Against the enemies hunting them, they needed all the help they could get. Peony had a point—unless he could somehow convince another witch to lend them aid, Miranda was their only hope. Even attempting to bargain with her was worth a shot, though he currently didn't have much to barter with.

"We should talk about this, Peony," he said. "In private."

"Go to bed, Bethaem," Peony said sharply. "We'll discuss this in the morning."

Beth had enough sense not to argue. With a growl of frustration, the girl whirled on her heel and stomped down the hall, making sure her every step could be heard.

"That girl." Peony clicked between her teeth. "I'd tan her hide with a whip if I thought it would change her any."

Atiernan couldn't help laughing. "No, that would just empower her more." Beth may have appeared meek at times, but he could tell she had the makings of a fierce and loyal warrior. He just hoped he lived to see it.

If the sentinels kept coming at this increased rate…anyone's survival was up in the air.

"I scried the creature we found by the gates," he admitted the second the girl was out of earshot.

Peony raised an eyebrow. "I'm assuming you didn't learn much. Or… You're worried by what you did discover."

There was no point in denying it. She could always see right through him.

"In the beast's recollections, I saw a man I didn't recognize."

"Could it be another witch come to rescue the one you captured?" Peony asked.

Atiernan hesitated. While he had implied as much to Miranda, he didn't think so. Male witches rarely strayed far from their harems. Besides, eyes that dark were the hallmark of a daemon.

"Atiernan?"

"I'm not sure," he admitted. "They didn't stick around for introductions."

"It could be a warning," Peony added. "Not that it matters. Someone is sending them, and they won't stop. We need to end this and fast."

She shot him a pointed glance, though he could read between the lines.

"Alright, old woman," he sighed. Ironically, frozen in youth, she looked years younger than he did. "I'll humor you this once. How does a man request the services of a witch who both hates and despises him *and* his people?"

Peony smiled. "For starters, you could begin by *not* threatening her life."

CHAPTER
FOUR

Miranda huddled in the corner of the main hall with all the dignity she could manage—which wasn't much. When Atiernan left, the other daemon had as well, leaving her alone near the slain sentinel. She wasn't foolish enough to think they'd forgotten about her. No.

Leaving her beside this beast was punishment enough for refusing their demands. The smell was repulsive, roiling her stomach. Even so, she didn't dare go searching for her cell again.

Sure, she may have survived days in confinement, but now…

The thought of darkness was suffocating. Until a few years ago, it and isolation had plagued her every waking moment. Despite growing up among the beautiful sacred forest surrounding Hazel's Way, she'd barely been allowed to enjoy the fresh air and run beneath the trees.

Not without a price to be paid.

You are a monster. Damned. To even live among us is a disgrace to the gods...

With a shudder, Miranda shook off the memories. She couldn't deny that, despite being a bound captive and stripped of her magic, she would rather wander the hall of her enemy than be shut away again. If that meant spending every second of freedom on edge, waiting for the moment the one they called *Atiernan* had no further use for her...

So be it.

They were going to kill her anyway. They *had* to, because she would rather die than give them what they wanted. She would never see her home again, or her family—not that those in the coven seemed to give a damn.

No one had come for her. Not a single witch.

As the daughter of the crone—the most honored member of the coven—an elite crew of the most gifted spellcasters should have beaten down the gates of Hell to retrieve her. In theory. The reality was a truth Miranda knew in her soul— no one would come, and certainly not at her mother's behest.

Trapped in Hell, she was as good as dead.

Still, she wouldn't offer the daemons any help. Their race was evil. Corrupted. If anyone knew as much, she did.

And no matter what anyone said, she was a witch first and foremost. Her loyalty to her coven was all she had left—and

Miranda knew in her soul that she would rather *die* than lose that too.

The time might come very soon to test that theory, she realized as a hulking shape appeared paces away.

Bathed in shadow, the towering figure advanced slowly, almost as if daring her to run.

And every cell in her body warned her to do just that.

Only one man possessed a frame so gloriously massive. Coiled muscle conveyed his intentions better than any verbal threat—he could gut her in seconds. Destroy her with those dexterous hands which seemed designed for that sole purpose. She wouldn't even be able to protect herself. Without her magic, she was nothing.

"Miranda." His voice rumbled like thunder, reverberating down to her very bones.

It was the first time he had referred to her by name, but hearing those syllables come from his mouth seemed more terrifying than anything she'd been presented with so far. It meant that she wasn't some nameless captive abducted on a whim. He'd taken time to learn something about her, if only that one detail.

Did he know more? Instinctively, she stumbled back until her body hit the firmness of the wall.

"W-What do you want?" Damn her for sounding so frightened. She certainly didn't mean to, for she was a Hazel witch after all.

But, gods…the man had fiery eyes. Almost bright enough to show her reflection. Not to mention the bloody shade of red hair draped over his shoulders. The hue alone served as a symbol of the carnage and gore he must have been responsible for.

Now she remembered his name and the horrific myth attached to it—Atiernan. A daemon so fearsome some of the vilest legends spawned from his deeds.

It didn't matter that he wore only a simple black shirt instead of blood-splattered mail. Or that a plain ring adorned his fingers instead of a gleaming sword.

This man was a warrior through and through. Miranda couldn't help but tremble as he came closer, setting every cell in her body on edge.

"C-Come to finally kill me?" she stammered.

Of course, she would be yet one more casualty added to the pile. How many other women had fallen prey to gleaming white teeth and strong hands? How many had been victimized by him in *other* ways? Against her will, that thought weaseled into her mind. Hundreds? Thousands?

Her only consolation was that she was way too plain to ever entice someone like him. Unlike her, he didn't seem to be mesmerized by *her* looks. His eyes were on the wall behind her.

"I'm not here to harm you," he said.

"The hell you aren't, daemon," she said icily. "If you want to kill me, then *kill* me. I'm not going to fight you."

She *couldn't* fight him, but that was beside the point.

"If you know what I am, then you know the damage I could do to you through magic alone," she added, merely to see the bastard squirm for once.

He didn't so much as twitch. Instead, the daemon's mouth convulsed into what might have been the semblance of a smile on another man. His teeth were far too sharp, however, and glistened wetly in the moonlight. "Don't tempt me, witch," he warned. "I have more important things to deal with than killing you."

"Oh?" Miranda couldn't suppress an involuntary gulp at the word choice. *Witch.* A joke? If so, he wasn't laughing. "I don't believe you," she gasped, flinching as he took another step forward. "Why else would you bring me here? I won't help you—"

"Then I shall just have to show you," Atiernan teased in a voice that was anything *but* teasing.

The look in his eyes was downright murderous—but all he did was muscle his way past her and approach another room across the hall.

"After you," he mocked in a voice of thunder. "Move quickly. I wouldn't want you to think that I might stab you in the back."

Miranda forced a dry swallow, and mustered what little strength she had left to walk past him and enter a room that held only a chair and a few simple pieces of furniture.

"See?" She flinched as Atiernan slipped inside behind her and slammed the door. "You've trusted me this far, and you are still alive."

"For now." Miranda whirled on him, unwilling to have the man out of her sight for even a moment—though his nearness was far too unsettling. Cautiously, she inched backward until the table's edge brushed her spine. Only then did she feel brave enough to continue, "But for you to rip me from my coven, and imprison me for days without explanation, I assume your motives extend far beyond a monster, daemon."

One fact alone emboldened her to speak to him so directly —the man wouldn't dare kill her here. Not without an audience to *watch* as he tore her apart. Right? She jumped as he advanced. He didn't reach for her, but what he did instead was no less threatening.

His eyes latched onto hers, rendering her immobile as he closed the distance remaining between them in a single step.

"Listen to me and listen good, woman," he growled. "I don't want to hurt you, but I *will* if you force me to."

His gaze swept over her entire body, leaving chills in its wake. Unable to suppress a shiver, she crossed her arms and fought to keep her sneer intact.

"Will you now?" she rasped. "Then I suggest you get on with it, daemon."

"Do not play with me, witch," he warned, matching her hostility tenfold. "Respect me *for what I am*, and I will respect you."

"Respect?" She threw her head back and laughed. "If you *respected* me, daemon, I wouldn't be in chains. My power would not be stripped, and you would not be asking me to do the one thing you know damn well I *cannot* do!"

The man blinked. For a long time, he only watched her, his gaze unreadable, before his upper lip curled back from his teeth.

"You are right," he said. "I *cannot* respect someone like you. Someone who would watch others die rather than help them out of some selfish, misplaced sense of pride."

He didn't shout—his tone was very, very quiet—but Miranda shied away from him anyway. Internally, however, she felt a tiny bit triumphant at having broken that icy cool.

This man may have frightened her, but he could not intimidate her. She would not change her mind, and she would make damn sure to let him know it.

"Go," she spat, trying to mimic his mocking tone. "I won't help you. I won't."

The man's gaze narrowed. "I know you believe that," he threw back.

"Then what do you want?" Miranda drew herself up to her full height, refusing to be caught off guard. The daemon seemed to be humoring her for a reason, and she intended to use the fact fully to her advantage.

Until he sighed, and his expression softened in a way that made her choke. "I want to make a deal," he said.

Wonder of wonders, he didn't seem to be joking.

His next words proved it.

"I came here to bargain with you. For your help, on your terms. I am not commanding your assistance. I'm asking for it."

"Bargain?" For a moment, all she could do was stare, before a mountain of hysterical laughter bubbled within her. Cackling maniacally, she collapsed against the table while her mind whirled as to what he could possibly mean.

It had to be a trick. But, glancing up through a haze of tears, she realized that the daemon wasn't laughing along with her.

"I do not play games, Miranda."

His words made her go silent, shoulders still shaking. Smirking, she tipped her head back and took him in with a single stare. Did he really expect her to believe that? She'd rather die than willingly use her magic for a daemon's bidding. Voice scathing, she told him so.

Only belatedly did she comprehend the true extent of what he was offering.

"I thought so—" Atiernan turned on his heel. In a blur of shadow, he was already at the door, ripping it open. "Beth was right. You are too much of a selfish *bitch* to ever be of use—"

"Wait!" Though a few hours ago, she would have never thought to do such a thing, Miranda found herself rushing across the room to stop him. He seemed shocked as well, and his eyes widened as they took her in.

"Wait," she repeated breathlessly. "I...I'm listening."

Atiernan watched her for the longest time, seeming to miss nothing with that haunting gaze. Then, all at once, he sighed and allowed the door to close once more.

"You're trying my patience, witch," he hissed, already back to not calling her by name. Why that simple realization stung, she didn't know.

Feeling lightheaded, she stumbled into the far corner of the room, where a simple chair waited, and collapsed onto it. "I'm listening," she repeated.

"I'll return some of your powers, witch, and see that you are released to your coven unscathed," he said finally. "*If*...you use them to help my pack defeat the sentinels."

Miranda raised an eyebrow. Well, the man certainly didn't waste any time. *All the better*, she thought calculatingly. His briskness just made him easier to fool.

"You want me to find out who is sending those creatures?" She heard herself reply.

"Yes. Help me against them, and I'll see that you are returned to your coven unharmed and your power restored."

The offer was tempting. The daemon had no idea just how much. The longer she suffered the darkness of his dungeon, the greater the risk she took. Gods, how she craved access to her natural magic. Without it, she could only delay the inevitable for so long...

The thought of regaining even a *fraction* of her powers was enough to make her do whatever the hell he wanted—but, after years of being used and taken advantage of, Miranda had learned nothing if not one thing—rarely did someone begin an offer with the most they were willing to give.

Start low and go high, went that old saying. Just how high was this Atiernan willing to go?

"Help you..." She stroked her chin. "How exactly?"

He smiled in a way that could shatter a dream into a nightmare.

"However I *order* you to, witch. If I tell you to throw yourself off a damn cliff and fly, you will."

Miranda shrugged, unwilling to divulge that if he *did* restore her powers, he wouldn't be able to *order* her to do anything. Better to let him think he had the upper hand.

"Will you return my powers immediately?"

"Some of them."

Damn. The man was good—not giving her an *inch* of room to negotiate. His tone warned her not to even try, but "some" was more than enough.

"If I agree?"

Atiernan frowned as if unsure whether she was toying with him or not. "Help me find who is sending the monsters after my people and why. In return, I will restore your powers and return you to your coven unharmed."

So his offer remained unchanged from before.

"Fair enough," Miranda agreed, though inside, she was crestfallen. Damn. It was too much to hope that he would return her magic first.

Even so. Power was still power...

"I'll help you, daemon," she said after a moment.

Cautiously, she stood.

"Really?" Atiernan didn't seem very pleased at having won this battle. In fact, he looked disgusted—the way one might look after making a deal with the devil.

"*Really*," she repeated mockingly. "I'll help your pack of degenerates if you just give me back my—"

Instantly, she knew it was the wrong thing to say. He lunged for her, gripping her neck in a single massive hand without warning. The next moment, she found herself lifted by her throat and *slammed* against the wall.

Miranda could only blink, dazed as his perfect face hovered mere inches from hers.

"Don't. You. *Ever*. Insult my people again." He snarled every word, one right after the other, before violently letting her go.

Ears ringing, Miranda slid gracelessly to the floor. Fear did funny things to a woman, she realized. Like, turning them into a silent, staring mass of terror that could only quiver at the foot of the enemy.

She waited for him to strike her...

He certainly looked angry enough to.

But, with a growl of disgust, Atiernan turned on his heel and barged through the doorway.

"Take her to the dungeons," she heard him snap to some unseen guard.

Then the door slammed shut behind him, leaving her alone to contemplate how close to death she'd just come.

CHAPTER
FIVE

The next morning, Miranda woke in hell.

The space was far too small. Too suffocating. She would never leave. Never. Not until she obeyed. Until she finally…

A sound jarred her from the memory, and she blinked, alarmed to find herself still enclosed but in a space far different than the prison she was used to. She stiffened, staring through the semi-darkness for a moment before she realized that she was not alone. Someone stood in the room with her…hovering above, like a living shadow.

She lunged from her pallet only to have a firm hand clasp over her mouth before she could even scream.

"It's me," came a deep, masculine voice.

Him. Helplessly, she looked up into a face carved from every woman's pure sexual fantasy, crowned by a head of blood-red hair. It was *him*.

Atiernan.

"W-What are you doing in here?" Her voice came out a breathless squeak as she scrambled into a corner.

Had he forgotten their bargain already? Or had he decided to just skip the niceties and kill her? Those piercing eyes, glittering like gems through the shadows, were unreadable, and Miranda couldn't help the ball of terror that took root in her chest.

If he did decide to harm her, there wouldn't be a damn thing she could do about it.

Not a damn thing at all...

"Come—"

He reached for her, and she recoiled with a cry—hands shielding her face—but the man gripped the back of her dress and hauled her forcefully to her feet.

"*Come,*" he repeated before leaving the cell without her.

Miranda couldn't stumble after him fast enough. She hated being locked in at night. Almost as much as she hated the dark...

The morning rays of sunlight streaming in through the windows on the upper level were a relief, and she huddled within the warmth. Watching Atiernan from the corner of her eye, she realized the comfort was a futile one.

"I trust you haven't forgotten your words from last night," the man said coldly.

From his casual, though hostile stance, the sunlight didn't affect him. Strange. Vampire legends, based on Raeths, were supposedly accurate for the most part. Sunlight, wood—all presumed to be the weaknesses of said daemons. Frankly, she didn't care to ask why he seemed immune. Though, *without* that ability, *he* would have been just as helpless during the day as *she* was locked in her cell at night.

The thought almost gave her a sick sort of pleasure until a small girl appeared near the edge of the hall. She was lithe, dressed in a gray pinafore, her long black hair in plaits.

That's right. This place was home not only to brooding, hulking men like Atiernan. Children lived here, and women too. Innocents who couldn't help that their men were violent brutes.

"She's ready, Atiernan," the girl said before darting away as quickly as she'd come—but not before pausing to shoot Miranda a dirty look.

It was only morning, and already the world was turned against her. *Fair enough*, she thought, rubbing her arms. Returning to Hazel's Way was her only focus. Either that, or dying with her dignity intact, which seemed a very unlikely goal as she caught sight of Atiernan glaring at her.

"Well, *do* you?"

"Y-yes," Miranda stammered. "I remember. My help in exchange for my safety and my magic."

The daemon grunted, seemingly satisfied by her response.

Up close, in the glaring light of day, he seemed no less formidable than he had in the dark. If she wasn't careful… and if he caught her so much as *thinking* to deceive him— the consequences would be deadly.

"Good," he replied. She had but a second's notice before he captured her wrist and turned, dragging her after him.

She stumbled. His touch was electric, dizzying, and sharp against her already-fragile skin. Damn…it had been so long since she'd had anyone—let alone a man—touch her. The sensation made her unconsciously long for human contact. Even her mother's unfeeling, empty caresses would have been enough. Gods, she hated being alone.

No. That was the delirium talking. The daemon's touch was as disgusting as ever. Nervously, her eyes darted up to the stern line of his jaw, watching as he pulled her surely through the winding hallways without looking back.

"Here."

She blinked to find herself shoved into a narrow room with rows and rows of dusty shelves, where a small woman knelt studiously over a bubbling cauldron.

"I brought her," Atiernan declared, before turning sharply on his heel and disappearing down the corridor.

"Good." The woman glanced up to scrutinize Miranda from behind the lenses of foggy glasses. "Come here and let me look at you."

She seemed young, early twenties perhaps. Her skin was eerily smooth, and her dark hair unmarred by even a speck of gray. Though, even with the absence of wrinkles, Miranda had enough sense to see through the façade. This woman was nowhere close to youthful, nor was she human.

"I'm Peony," she said, revealing a flash of sharp fangs as she inspected Miranda from head to toe. It didn't seem to faze her that Atiernan was gone. "You must be the witch I've heard so much about."

"My *name* is Miranda." Miranda stayed near the room's threshold. She didn't like the way the woman was watching her—as if she knew all her secrets and then some. "Would *you* like it if *I* referred to you as daemon?"

Peony smiled coldly. "Many of your kind do." For a moment, she held Miranda's gaze with those haunting eyes. Then, without a word, she turned back to her bubbling brew. Every few seconds, she glanced at Miranda again, her expression unreadable.

"Are you part of the bargain?" Miranda finally wondered. Was she supposed to help this strange woman somehow?

Whatever the answer, the woman didn't reply. She only continued to stir the contents of her cauldron with a slender silver rod pulled from the bell of her sleeve.

Miranda watched, unintentionally noting everything the woman was doing wrong. From the spicy scent tickling her nose, the potion was a strong one and well-crafted at that. While not a witch, the woman must have been a formidable brewer.

But this current brew was missing something—not to mention that silver shouldn't be used to stir the concoction but wood. And not just any wood, but *white wood* to lend the potion strength via the nature from which it drew its power.

If Peony was bothered by her staring, she didn't show it. Instead, she pointed to a small vial on a nearby shelf.

"Grab that, would you?"

Miranda hesitated. This woman worked for Atiernan—not to mention was a daemon—and damn well couldn't be trusted. But, if she were part of Atiernan's bargain, she had no choice.

Carefully, she forced herself to enter the room and grabbed the requested vial. Then she approached the woman and relinquished the bottle to her pale grasp.

She stood back, expecting the woman to ignore her once more, but Peony surprised her by jerking her head up from her brew and staring intently at her with those ancient eyes.

"How much should I use?" the daemon wondered aloud.

Miranda answered without thinking. "It depends on however much *Raven's sleeve* you added."

Rubbing her chin, she thought to recall the correct calculation. It had been so long since she'd brewed her own potions, but the work was familiar and relaxing. Already, she felt her shoulders tense with the welcome complexity of solving a problem.

"Well," Peony began thoughtfully, "I think half a handful."

"Oh." Miranda shook her head. "You'll need *much* more than that." Frowning, she approached the cauldron and crouched as close to the daemon as she dared.

Absently, she tied her hair into a haphazard bun while her nose did the work she'd trained for since her days as a young girl peering over her mother's shoulder. When the woman could bear her nearness, that is...

One image, in particular, came to mind. She'd been six or seven, desperate to learn the ways of potion crafting, so she watched her mother from an unseen corner. She must have moved suddenly because the woman spotted her.

And the resulting beating left bruises that took weeks to heal.

At the memory, she winced and almost missed what the daemon said next.

"I assume you have a suggestion," Peony prodded.

"Yes." Miranda refocused her attention on the mage. "You'll need at least twice as much if you're brewing what I think you are."

Peony glanced at her shrewdly. "And what is that?"

Miranda smiled, confident she could recognize the concoction only by smell. "Conjuring potion," she said, unsurprised when the daemon nodded in confirmation.

"Not just any conjuring potion," she went on. "But the *blackspeth*."

It was one of the strongest brews of its kind. If the daemon had come so close to forming it on her own, then...against her will, Miranda was impressed. Few witches could achieve the same result through trial and error despite having countless spell books and ingredients at their disposal.

She knew firsthand how hard it was to learn magic that way. Potions especially took intense dedication to measure the ingredients just right, not to mention enough patience to stir the concoction for however many days it took to form.

"Oh? Then if that is the case, what am I doing wrong?" Peony challenged. "I could see you frowning from here. Will you reveal your secrets, witch?"

The woman released a dry chuckle that reminded Miranda of the old crones at Hazel's Way, humoring a young upstart who thought she knew all the answers.

But in this case, Miranda was confident that she *did*.

Despite everything, she eagerly returned Peony's playful grin.

"Let's start with the *Raven's sleeve* first," she said, spotting a pile of the herb on a nearby table. Pulling up her sleeves, she stood to fetch it. "Then I'll explain the importance of stirring with *wood*..."

CHAPTER
SIX

After hours of attending to the daily tasks involved with running his fortress, Atiernan dreaded returning to the storeroom. While Peony may have requested the witch's help, he fully expected to find Miranda in pieces on the blood-splattered floor. Near the space in question, he caught sight of Beth instead, peering through the doorway. Once again, her fangs were protruding.

"It's horrible," she growled under her breath. "Awful."

"Oh?" Atiernan steeled himself for whatever grisly scene might await him.

Miranda, torn to pieces, while Peony stood over her with blood-smeared fangs?

The first scenario seemed likely, as he turned to find the mage indeed standing over the witch while brandishing a dangerous-looking knife. He could only watch, throat tight, as Peony brought the blade down…

To cleanly slice through the thick, monstrous-looking root Miranda held between her palms. The root split easily, and a dark liquid dribbled out to join the mixture frothing in the cauldron.

"You see?" the witch was explaining. At least, he *assumed* it was Miranda, for her lips were moving, but he hardly recognized her voice without the cutting edge of hate. "Slicing the *pherrus root* like this will produce more oil and reduce the waste."

"Ah," Peony exclaimed, throwing her head back with a mischievous cackle. "A good thing too, for I'm close to running out. You don't want to know what I had to do to get the stock I have now."

Atiernan knew. Peony had single-handedly infiltrated a coven of warlocks and stolen whatever she could—but not without killing the few who dared to get in her way.

Miranda didn't ask, but Atiernan could tell from her wary frown that the woman already knew enough of the daemon to guess that she hadn't gotten her supplies through entirely legal means.

"It can be quite expensive," the witch agreed instead. "Which is why the trick is to always save the husk." As she spoke, her pale hands worked to wrap the two ends of the bulbous root in a kerchief. "You can always dry them, grind them, and then boil the powder to produce just as much, *if not more,* oil than they contained. If the process is done right."

"Aha!" Peony cackled even more gleefully than before. "To think! All this time, I've been using the horrible things to fertilize my garden."

Miranda laughed as well, and the two women began to rummage through a pile of assorted roots in companionable silence.

"They've been like this, *all day*," Atiernan heard Beth mutter in awe. "All day. Just chatting and working as if they were damn *bosom buddies*."

"Beth," Atiernan scolded, though he feared the girl was right. Watching Miranda and Peony—two women who should have despised each other—working casually with herbs and potions...

They did seem, to put it plainly, like *"damn bosom buddies."*

Though not for long if he had any say in it.

"Witch—" His tone came out harsher than intended as he entered the room, glaring accusingly at Peony.

Miranda jumped, her dark eyes flitting to the mage as if she expected the woman to defend her. Which, to Atiernan's great surprise, she seemed willing to do.

"I expect you'd want her to call *you* by name, Atiernan," the daemon began coldly. "So, I suggest you begin with calling *Miranda* by hers."

"Oh?" Atiernan raised an eyebrow.

There were many ways he could respond to Peony's suggestion. Such as the fact that he could have called anyone anything he damned well pleased—this was his house on his territory, after all. But he knew Peony would sooner beat him over the head with the knife she still clenched than allow him to admit it.

So, with a growl of annoyance, he spat out the name through gritted teeth. "Miranda—"

"Better," Peony praised with a nod, clapping her pale hands. "After a few thousand years, I knew that I'd have beaten manners into you, yet."

Atiernan glared, annoyed that Miranda was there to witness him being scolded like a wayward child.

By the gods, he thought tiredly, reaching up to rub his throbbing temples. If Peony wasn't the closest thing he had to a mother, he'd…

"You came just in time," Peony went on smugly, well aware of his embarrassment. "*Miranda* was just finishing going over the finer points of potion crafting."

"Oh?" Atiernan couldn't help the suspicious edge to his tone. He didn't trust Miranda and the word "potion" in the same sentence. No doubt, the witch had been brewing a *poison* designed to kill them all. "What kind of potion?"

Peony smiled gleefully. "The *blackspeth*."

"The *blackspeth*?" Atiernan blinked, unable to hide his confusion. "I thought you perfected that brew months ago?"

Peony flashed a mischievous grin. "Oh, dear. You've blown my cover, Atiernan." She chuckled, eyeing Miranda, who looked just as confused as he felt.

"I-I thought…" Slowly, comprehension dawned on the witch, and she scoffed.

"I've fooled you, yes," Peony admitted, seemingly unashamed. "But I have also learned so much—so much!"

In fact, the mage seemed to glow with her new knowledge. Triumphantly, she clasped her hands and met Atiernan's shocked stare with a grin. "You must bring her back tomorrow."

With that, she stooped to gather the cauldron in her arms and scurried to another corner of the room. The bulky metal bowl seemed far too large for a woman of her size to carry without help, but Peony did so easily. With a jaunty cackle, she slipped past them and out of the room.

"Bring her back," she repeated, before disappearing down the hall, making no mistake that she wanted this strange partnership to continue.

"She tricked me." Miranda stared after Peony with something that might have been hurt flashing in those brown eyes. "She *tricked* me."

"Don't be so sure," Atiernan heard himself mutter, though he felt no desire to comfort the witch. In truth, Peony had done more to fool *him* than her. "It took her years to perfect that potion," he admitted. "And even still, it rarely worked as it should."

If Peony's good mood was anything to go by, with the witch's help, she had finally mastered the conjuring potion to its fullest capability. For that fact alone, he couldn't help but feel some tiny, twisted, glimmer of admiration.

Until he saw the bitch's loathing stare aimed in his direction.

"I should have expected as much," she snarled. "From *your* kind, what else is there to expect but dirty tricks? What next? You have me sacrifice that little girl to teach you the ins and outs of blood rites? Such a practice must be a casual affair for you Raeths."

The insult alone wasn't what sent rage roaring through Atiernan, blinding him to reason. It was her tone. Without another thought, he reached for her, capturing her neck in one hand. His grip was harsh, nails piercing tender flesh as he hauled her to her feet. He heard her whimper, such a faint, fearful little thing that reminded him just how afraid of him she truly was.

As if stung, he released her throat in favor of her forearm, though his grip was no less harsh.

"Go to your mother, Beth," he snapped as the girl watched him manhandle the witch down the opposite end of the corridor.

When he reached the cell they kept her in, he threw her inside, prepared to slam the door and lock her in—but, before he could, a pale hand reached from the shadows to grasp his chest.

"Please don't close it all the way," the witch croaked. "Not in the dark. *Please!* Not in the dark…"

She shouldn't have touched him. As if trapped in another man's body, he stared down at the slim fingers entangled in the fabric of his shirt. Felt her heat. Heard the tempting swish of her pulse.

The sound was a melody, playing on the darker impulses he strived to keep in check. Lured to the surface by blood, Atiernan couldn't fight instinct any longer.

In a matter of seconds, he pushed his way into that narrow room, causing Miranda to stumble back as the door slammed behind them.

Good gods…*her scent.* It hit him like a punch. Unchecked, his fangs slid painfully from their sheaths to pierce his bottom lip, but by then, he was already lunging toward her as she tried in vain to run.

"No, *please*," she whimpered, but her terror only aroused the predator he was.

She might as well have tried to reason with a wolf—her pleas would have fared better then. Every cell, bone, and muscle in his body had been crafted to fit the demanding needs of an apex predator. He couldn't fight it, couldn't resist. In a heartbeat, he had her against the wall, trapped between his body and the hard stone. Roughly, he tilted her head to the side, pinning her hips with his to keep her immobile. Hell, she could scarcely *breathe* as he dipped his head to inhale the heavenly aroma drifting from that throat.

Easy, a part of him scolded. It had been so damn long since he'd taken fresh blood right from the vein…

He could hurt her if he wasn't careful—and he didn't want to. That much was surprisingly clear, the only coherent thought he could muster. He didn't want to hurt her.

And the witch didn't want to be bitten. She squirmed, her pulse a frantic swish of churning blood. The desperation of the display shocked him. They kept willing humans in the manor for a reason, and, like Sanna, they weren't under duress and frankly weren't hard to find. Most knew of the pleasure sowed by the bite of a Raeth.

Though, she was a witch. Disgust of the act was promoted among her kind. From birth, they were taught their blood was pure, desired by all daemons, and to relinquish even a drop was to forfeit their very soul. When her lips parted, he expected her to preach as much and steeled himself for a lecture on purity.

"No. You don't… I'm not… I won't taste right," she squeaked. "I'm…bad. Tainted. You don't want me. I have corrupted blood—"

"Liar," he snarled, lowering his nose until the tip pressed into her delicate flesh.

A plea, yes, that would have made him withdraw. Not this callous ploy. A witch deny her own purity? Bullshit. Especially when she was so obviously wrong. Her scent grew stronger, making his mouth water with the potency. If she tasted even remotely like it…

With a growl of hunger, he spread his lips against that warm skin, and without hesitation, he bit as gently as someone like him could. He would take just a drop. A sample, no more.

He had refrained from the practice for so long. One small lapse in sobriety wouldn't hurt, and as his prize dripped onto his tongue, he felt not one ounce of guilt. Hot and sweet, her blood filled his mouth, and Atiernan couldn't silence a groan.

She was telling the truth—she didn't taste anywhere near what he imagined.

No. She was too exquisite for words, dangerously decadent.

One drop became another, which became another. Then another bite to add to the flow. More.

He'd stop soon, he told himself. *Soon.*

But as her body went limp, he sank to the floor, cradling her tiny form against his lap.

And then he fed again, more ravenously.

He'd stop soon. He would…

But deep down…

He knew he *couldn't* stop himself. Not until he drained her dry.

CHAPTER
SEVEN

Stop! The command ripped through his brain, belonging to the one shred of self-control he had left. It alone allowed him to withdraw and suck in lungfuls of fresh air. For as long as he could, he kept himself from gazing down at the witch resting in his arms. She wasn't dead. Not yet.

If he didn't control himself soon, however, she would be. Damn. When had he last fed with such abandon? Too long to recall. He refused blood even from the willing humans on the manor grounds and never directly from the vein. The long abstinence could partly explain his lapse in judgment —but not entirely. Good gods, her taste was like nothing he'd ever...

The adjectives flooded his mind, more poetic than he typically deigned to be. Her flavor was raw and powerful, daunting and sweet.

Decadent.

Each delicious drop tore through his veins, alighting every cell with a need for more. And more, and more, and *more*. Hungrily, he returned to her throat and bit down again, sending his fangs deep into that tender flesh, relishing the warm wash of blood that followed.

As if from far away, he heard her whimper, and instantly, terror clouded her taste, souring it.

He cursed. He had never enjoyed the taste of fear when he fed, and in her, it was revolting—like mud sullying the finest wine. In disgust, he withdrew his fangs with a bloody *pop*.

"I won't hurt you." His voice rasped in a way he didn't recognize. A monster was speaking, not him. Though, he hadn't always played the role of a proper, decent daemon lord.

There was a time when he would have pinned her down and fed until she ceased to breathe.

But no more.

"You taste like heaven, witch." He nuzzled her neck, inclined to soothe her fear the only way he knew how. Logic and reason were gone—only instinct remained. Seduction was a game he hadn't played in millennia, but with her blood as the prize, he was suddenly willing to try. "I won't hurt you. My bite can be enjoyed if you relax. I'm sure you realize that."

A shudder ran through her, betraying that she'd heard the rumors after all. Still, she seemed tense beyond all reason, and he knew fear had nothing to do with it. His nostrils flared as he fought to decipher the elusive emotion tinging her blood. Shame?

To be sure, he gripped her waist with one hand, using the other to cup her ribcage, sensing the delicate heart hammering madly beneath. The frantic sound gave him more context—she wasn't horrified of him, but...embarrassed.

Perhaps her words weren't lies. She believed them. The witches must have changed their tactics to prevent their women from allowing daemons to feed from them. No longer did they proudly deem their race to be superior above all. They were taught that they themselves were tainted.

A laugh trickled from his throat. The sound startled the witch so badly, she stopped resisting. Instead, her hands flew to his shoulders, her nails biting deep.

"No more, please," she rasped. "You'll hurt. You don't understand. I'm not—"

"You are perfection." His voice grated in a way he didn't recognize, but he meant every word—more sincerely than he wanted her to know. "I have never tasted anyone like you. So sweet... Let me feed, and you won't regret it. I can pleasure you..."

Without hesitation, he let his hand inch higher, and a guttural sound tore from his chest the moment a globe of flesh eagerly filled his palm. Her heat taunted him, almost as enticing as her blood. Unchallenged, he couldn't help himself. His thumb found a raised peak beneath the fabric of her dress—a small breast—and he stroked it, roughly...*slowly*...

A gasp tore from her throat, not a scream. Curious, he slid his tongue over the still bleeding fang marks, deciphering the unique flavor of the drops that escaped her next.

Telltale notes of pleasure mingled with her intoxicating taste, spurring his hunger to a painful degree. At the same time, the lust served as an anchor, allowing him to regain some small shred of control.

Fucking was another carnal pleasure he'd denied himself, but he was willing to make yet another exception. If sensual touch kept the witch open to having her blood taken, it could only be seen as a "win-win."

"Trust me, witch," he murmured against her pulse point. "Give me more, and you won't regret it. I can make you feel far better than my venom coursing through your veins does."

He knew it was a futile ask—no self-respecting witch would ever submit to him willingly.

But this one seemed determined to thwart his expectations at every turn. Her head fell back, exposing more of her throat to him, and he grunted in surprise. Then, he tweaked that erect nipple with his thumb and sucked at the flowing stream of blood.

Better, he thought in between deep, ravenous gulps. Much, *much* better. The first taste, even sullied by pain and fear, had been exquisite, but this…

With every bit of contact, she shivered. Shuddered. Panted. He knew she'd deny it later, but pride alone couldn't disguise the pleasure singing through her veins. Gingerly, his hand continued to manipulate her breast as he settled her against his lap, her thighs on either side of him.

"Relax," he coaxed as she stiffened. "I can make you feel even better than this…"

His other hand inched down her hip, ghosting between her legs. The male in him appreciated that she wore only a pair of cotton panties beneath her dress—fabric that felt like tissue paper as he teased her with the tip of his thumb.

It had been years since his last lay. Thankfully, the scent of a warm, willing woman brought every suppressed urge roaring to the surface.

And this witch certainly seemed willing. She was so damn hot, her mound soft beneath a thatch of curling hair, easily parted with a nudge of his probing finger. At the slightest bit of contact, she quivered and issued a gasp against his ear. It was all the encouragement he needed to prod her again, with more pressure. More. Over and over, until her flavor brimmed with sweetness—almost too much to bear all at once.

If only she would relinquish the shame that still flavored her. Even half-dumb with his venom circling her veins, the woman still had her damn pride.

"You have nothing to be ashamed of, witch," he rasped, surfacing from her blood once again. "If you relax…"

He stroked her once again, and there was no need to elaborate.

After all, he could sense the unconscious need no good witch would ever admit. The craving for contact. Nearness. Intimacy. It had been a long, long while since she'd had a man touch her like this. Try as she might, her body couldn't deny its own hunger—she ached. Ached to have a man fill her, even his thumb would suffice.

Oh yes, the witch knew all too well just what he promised, and her eyes flew up to meet his. The brown orbs were swollen with doubt and alarm—but no fear. Inch, by precious inch, he felt her body relax, no longer shying from his touch. And, true to his promise, Atiernan slid his thumb deep into her warmth.

She whined, gasping for air, but he barely heard her. Her muscles went rigid around him, and he groaned at the sensation. By the gods, she was a tight fit. So very damn *tight*—but, as his fingers thrust deep, she eagerly spread for him.

More than eagerly.

Her channel rippled in a rhythmic press of muscle, urging him deeper. In no uncertain terms, the slender sheath begged to be filled by something much larger than mere fingers. *Mmmm,* he thought darkly. He would make her scream…

"Atiernan!"

The distant voice dragged him from the heat of bloodlust and back into the cold, harsh reality. One where he was currently in the middle of a dark room, with none other than a bleeding witch crushed against him.

All because he lost control like a damned animal.

Guilt hit him like a blow to the gut. Dazed, he released her, lurching to his feet as footsteps rushed down the corridor, coming dangerously close to her cell.

He could still taste her blood on his tongue. His hands…

"Atiernan! Are you in here?"

"I'm here. I'll meet you upstairs." Lust pounded painfully in his gut as he swiped the blood from his chin with the back of his hand before heading to the door.

He didn't look back at her—he couldn't. But he could *hear* her, panting as she rode the final peals of pleasure neither of them could deny.

Whether intentionally or not, he left the door open on his way out, allowing the dim light of the hall to lessen the darkness she feared so much.

Atiernan entered the main hall to find it empty, but worried voices reached him, echoing off the walls.

"Where the hell is he? Atiernan!"

"Perhaps he is still in the dungeon—?"

"I'm here," Atiernan spoke just as he rounded the corner, coming face to face with a group of his men.

"Thank the heavens," Benjamin snapped. "It's about damn time… There's blood on you, my lord."

"What?" Atiernan angrily swiped at his mouth with the back of his hand. Damn, he could still taste her. "I was with a human," he lied.

Benjamin raised an eyebrow, but kept the location he found his lord to himself. "Peony says she needs us. All of us—it's urgent."

"Lead the way," Atiernan ordered, inclining his head. He could feel the others watching him, their eyes lingering over the scarlet liquid on his chin and the strain at the front of his slacks.

He didn't pray to any divine entity, and yet the phrase most mortals uttered seemed fitting in this instance—gods above. What the hell had she done to him? Could a woman like *Miranda* be cunning enough to seduce *him*? No, he realized, thinking back. It had been the other way around—he had seduced her, or come damn close. He couldn't help himself —the moment he smelled her scent...

Thousands of years of careful restraint, and in one fell swoop, the predator he truly was had risen to the surface. And damn, it had been *delicious* losing control. Perfect. Wild. *Wrong.*

He'd always thought killing would trigger his old instincts —not the throaty pleasure of a witch. Nothing would have pleased him more in the entire world than going back to her and finishing what he'd started by draining the wench dry. Even though his cock throbbed longingly to do just that, he knew without a doubt it was impossible.

The next time he came so close to Miranda, it would have to end with her dead. Or in chains. Or *something*. Granted, it was a surprise to discover just how lusty the woman could be, when she seemed so plain and prudish and...empty. Damn, she needed to be fucked. And not just fucked, but ravished, lusted, torn apart—by him. *He* needed to have her, *claim* her.

"Atiernan?"

"Yes?" He blinked, surprised to find Benjamin standing before him.

"Are you alright?" the man asked.

"Fine," he snapped, annoyed for reasons he couldn't explain. "You said Peony asked for me?"

"Yes," Ben said with a nod. "She asked for all of us. I don't know why."

The thought made him wary. Peony wasn't the type to call group gatherings for the hell of it. Usually, the mage was quite content to lock herself in her storeroom and spend the day brewing potions rather than socializing.

In fact, the few times he could remember her ever having to gather his men had not ended well.

"Hmm."

Intrigued, he headed down the hall, where a crowd gathered around a doorway. Craning his neck, he could make out the thin shape of Peony, surveying his men with a shrewd expression. When she saw him, her eyes narrowed, and she beckoned him closer.

"I'll have a word with you, Atiernan. In private."

Uneasy, he muscled his way into the room, and Peony closed the door behind him.

"What is it?"

The mage looked uncharacteristically grim, and he didn't like how her eyes flashed from behind those dirty glasses.

"The sentinels," she said simply. "At least that is what I assume they are. Look—" She turned to a table that Atiernan could see was laden with weapons and a large map. "Our scouts have caught word from the east of at least twelve creatures…headed our way."

Damn, Atiernan thought with a hiss. "When?" he demanded, already lurching toward the door. His people needed to be warned, the territory fortified, not to mention the damn witch secured.

If the invaders weren't the sentinels—and witches instead—Miranda couldn't be trusted anywhere near the perimeter. It would be better for everyone to release her now, before she became a bigger liability.

"The news came hours ago," Peony admitted while palming a slender knife. "I waited until now to tell you, but I wanted to be sure."

"Where is the breach," he snarled, eyes flashing already with battle-lust. He dared any of the sentinels—or any of his enemies for that matter—to attack him now. *Now,* when he felt enraged enough to tear hoards of the bastards apart with plenty of wrath left to spare.

"Where?" he repeated when Peony didn't reply. He whirled on the mage to find her watching him with an unreadable expression.

"From the mountains," she said finally. "If it is the sentinels, it should take them no sooner than three days to reach us."

"Three days. That's nothing!" Atiernan gritted his teeth at the possibility. Hell, they'd be lucky to have the perimeter secured before morning. Miranda would have to wait another day to gain her freedom.

If they managed to live that long…

"We should prepare," Peony said. "Though, if we can convince the witch to help us sooner, we might not need to risk a full assault."

She had a point though Atiernan loathed to admit it. Damn the witch. If there was one thing he knew how to do without the aid of magic and tricks, it was fight. Witch or no witch, they would survive this encounter. He barreled into the hall while mentally reviewing battle tactics—and nearly ran over someone in the process.

"Lord Atiernan—"

The husky purr was not the fear-laced whimper of Miranda. Startled, he drew back, taking in the slender, female form with a grudging hint of admiration. Sanna, who'd changed since their last encounter. Her hair hung loose down to her hips, though the strands strategically avoided covering the rosy nipples clearly visible beneath the fabric of a tight dress the color of blood. Her green eyes watched him, alight with a hunger he knew all too well.

"Sanna." He tried his hardest to hide his annoyance as he attempted to pass her.

Giggling, she blocked him.

"You seemed worried, my lord." The statement was innocent, but the tone was not.

The part of him, still aroused by Miranda's scent, stirred at the husky whisper. Objectively, the woman was beautiful, even for a mortal. She'd come to his fortress over a year ago via whatever channels they used to solicit willing feeders. From the rumors, he knew she eagerly satisfied the hunger —and other appetites—of the males among his pack. There was a time when Atiernan would have gladly sampled her many wares. No more. After a few thousand years, he was well past the age when he could easily be blinded by beauty, unable to see the real creature underneath.

Liva had been beautiful as well, beyond mortal comprehension.

In the end, she had been the same breed of woman that he knew Sanna was. The vicious, ambitious type willing to do anything or *anyone* for power. Their beauty was just the weapon they used to achieve their end.

But what did that make *Miranda*? She didn't ooze sex in the way Liva and Sanna both did, but with one little whimper...

A thousands-year-old warrior had risen to the surface, hungry only for her.

With one little moan...

She'd nearly had him undone.

He lost himself in the memory of her in his arms, sweet and warm and so damn soft. His cock stirred, urging him to find her and finish what they'd started. God, at the mere thought of her, he was steel. Aching. He didn't even hear Sanna speak until he saw her red lips moving in slow motion.

"W-what?"

"Oh, my Lord." With a flick of her gaze, she inspected the front of his pants, and her plump lips curved into a ripe grin. "I wanted to know if you needed help…securing the perimeter?"

The seductive way she ran a hand down her hip next warned that she wasn't referring to the "perimeter" of the manor. Her green eyes darkened with a sensual lust that made something inside him lurch.

Though he damn well knew better than to toy with a woman like her.

"Where did you hear that?" he demanded, unable to help the gruff tone. It wouldn't do him any good if rumors of the sentinels slipped free and started a panic.

Sanna just gave him another knowing smile. "I have my ways."

Boldly, she ran a finger down his chest, and Atiernan had to smother a frown as her sharp nails nicked his skin through the fabric of his shirt.

He could guess as to her "ways," alright, and had the sudden urge to tan the hide of whichever one of his men had decided that pleasing his cock was worth divulging sensitive information.

"But, what about the witch—"

"Huh?" At the mention of Miranda, Atiernan's senses were torn in two completely different directions. The first, driven by logic, was an impulsive desire to make sure she was secure in her cell—and nowhere near the perimeter in case the witches had come for her after all and not the sentinels.

At the same time, his nostrils flared, aching for that enticing scent, and it was a struggle to keep his balance as the world started to sway. He barely even saw Sanna as he pushed past her, suddenly determined to find the witch. He'd left the door to her cell unlocked, and a part of him almost wished that she had been stupid enough to seize her freedom by leaving the dungeon.

If so, he would take immense pleasure in hunting her down.

"Atiernan."

He'd barely gone a step before Peony's voice rang out behind him. He turned to find the mage watching him from a doorway, gray eyes unusually wary.

"Bethaem ran off again—" She shrugged, as if unconcerned, but Atiernan could tell from her tone that she was worried. "The girl barely stays where I tell her to anymore. If you come across her, send her to our room," she added. "I don't want her getting in anyone's way."

"Of course." Atiernan nodded. He shared Peony's concern.

Until they discovered just who or what had managed to skirt their perimeter, then the halls of the manor weren't safe for anyone, be they daemon or witch.

CHAPTER
NINE

The daemons were stirring throughout the great house, and Miranda jumped with every thud and shout to penetrate the quiet of the dungeon. The sounds reminded her all too well that, without her power, she was no more than a human in their midst.

And humans could easily find themselves destroyed in the chaos of battle—because there could be only one explanation for the sudden tension.

Those monsters. The sentinels…

Fear pierced her like a knife sinking deep as she pictured an alive version of the monstrosity Atiernan had her inspect. For a moment, she forgot that she was currently huddled against the wall, with blood dripping down her neck.

Oh, dear heavens. With a start, she returned to her senses and pressed a hand to the side of her throat. Two pin-prick marks pierced the flesh—but the dull, physical pain was *nothing* in the face of shame.

No wonder the witches in her coven hated her so. One daemon had proved the grim reality Miranda had always tried to ignore—she was different.

Corrupted.

She wouldn't think of what the warrior had done to her. Wouldn't think of what *she* had done in return—letting him…

Instead, she mustered what little dignity she had left to wrestle her dress down over her legs. Without a mirror, there wasn't much she could do about the blood on her neck. Even still, she tried to wipe the warm liquid away with the back of her hand—but it coated her.

She could smell it, but it was nothing compared to the unmistakable feeling of her body's own arousal, wetting the skin between her legs.

It had been so long since anyone had ever touched her like that. Hell, *no one* had ever touched her like that. She *wouldn't* think of it—wouldn't think of him. Desperate, she took a step, trying to ignore the blossoming heat…

A sudden thump made her jump, her heart pounding. Was it Atiernan, come to finish what he started? No. She caught sight of a figure lurking out of view behind the open door to her cell and breathed a sigh of relief. They were far too thin to be the warrior.

"Who's there?" she called.

The intruder attempted to remain hidden, but as Miranda crept to the mouth of her cell, she caught sight of the culprit retreating down the hall.

"You," she rasped, spotting the man who'd been near the monster Atiernan had brought her to see. "Has he sent you to make sure I obeyed his order like a good captive?"

Damn. She didn't mean to sound quite so bitter and hateful—the wrath wasn't even directed at the man, she admitted, but at herself. She had never hated herself quite so much—and after all she'd been through, there had been plenty of opportunities.

"And if I am?" the man snarled, turning to face her. "If Atiernan won't watch you, I will."

Miranda blinked. Then she remembered the bloody marks on her neck and scrambled back to the shadows. She'd rather lose what little pride she had left than admit she'd been fed on by a daemon.

"I don't need a babysitter," she forced herself to reply. "If Ater—If *he* wants me secured, then you'd better go tell him to *lock me in!*"

"Fine," the man countered, taking a step. "Have it your way—"

Ha! Miranda would have laughed out loud if she wasn't already so shaken. As it was, she could barely hide a frightened whimper as the man reached for the door to her cell.

"Wait!" She hated how pathetic she sounded. "I…I need to use the bathroom."

At least she'd have the chance to wipe away the blood.

She rushed by the daemon before he could refuse, though she knew he followed. Drenched in fear, she raced up the steps and peeked into the main hall. It appeared empty...so far. Not even a spider scurried in view. It was as if every living creature had been scared off by the rousing clamor of Atiernan and his men.

But even they had gone silent, she realized, straining her ears. You could hear a pin drop—it was so damn quiet. Cautiously, she took a step into the hall, relishing the fresh air and soft sunlight that washed over her from a nearby window.

"Benjamin!" The voice drew her notice down the hall where another man stood, his gaze on the daemon behind her. "You're needed."

The man, Benjamin, scoffed. "The bathroom is that way. Stray anywhere else, and you will pay the price," he snarled at Miranda before stalking off.

She watched him round the corner and leave her view. Feeling bold, she took another step, heading blindly in the opposite direction. This part of the corridor was long and curving, dotted with countless doors leading to even more rooms.

Her only consolation was that a place this size had to have more than one bathroom. There was a bucket in her cell that she used when the threat of soiling herself outweighed the shame of feeling like a prisoner—but even daemons had to relieve themselves somewhere...

She paused before a random door and twisted the door-knob. A quick peek inside revealed not a bathroom, but a bedroom instead. A massive one, with plenty of large, pristine windows gleaming to display the morning sky.

It didn't even look lived in—the bed was neatly made and the floor cold. Apparently, a lack of available space wasn't the reason she'd been shoved into the dungeon. It was only when she had the sense to go inside one of those rooms that she realized each one had a connecting bathroom.

Every single one. And they weren't small and cramped like her own room back home, but large and full and luxurious.

Why, if she currently wasn't a captive, she would have torn off her clothes and soaked inside the huge, gleaming bathtub found in one of the suites. As it was, she only ducked within a cupboard for a plush washcloth and a measly bar of soap to attack her filthy, sweaty skin. She didn't dare look in the mirror—she couldn't.

Instead, she worked blindly, wetting the washcloth in warm water from the tap and dragging it over her aching skin. She wished she could rip it off—tear her own hide from her body—and get a new one clean and renewed.

Unfortunately, even if she had access to her magic, such a transformation wouldn't be possible, and she had to settle for soap instead. After the first pass, the cloth came away spotted with dried blood, and the sight of it did her in. All at once, she collapsed against the side of the bathtub, hunched over the rim.

She hated herself. More than ever before—*hated* every single thing about her body. Most of all, she hated the treacherous ache pooling between her thighs. An ache that burned whenever she thought of the daemon —*desiring* him even though she should have despised him.

Why did he have to drink her blood?

She wished he would have choked. Recoiled in disgust. Anything but rasp that she tasted like…perfection. Why give her the memories of him hot and heavy at her throat?

To intimidate her? To haunt her dreams as he did this waking nightmare?

Whatever his reasons, she hated him for it. Loathed him. The man wouldn't kill her, or physically harm her, but somehow the sting of his fangs piercing her flesh had hurt worse than any torture. So much worse.

Because, deep in her soul, she knew that she only wanted to feel that sweet agony again.

And again, and again, and *again*.

Pull yourself together, she thought, pushing back from the rim of the tub to stand on her feet.

She was a Hazel witch, damn it! Why wasn't she acting like one?

After wiping the tears away, she forced herself to face the mirror and gasped. The reflection belonged to a stranger. A woman with frightfully pale skin and black, gaping shadows for eyes and tangled brown hair stuck to the side of her neck by a sheen of blood.

That couldn't possibly be her. Dazed, she pushed a curl from her face, and the mirror-woman did the same, horror blossoming over her expression. To make matters worse, more blood slowly dribbled down her shoulder to dot the tile beneath her feet.

Eyes closing, she turned away, knowing the truth as it came to hit her—she wasn't brave. Far from it, but she'd be *damned* if she didn't survive this mess and come out alive. It would take more than a daemon warrior to break her down.

Reaching for the light switch, she flicked it off and scurried back into the hall.

She'd barely gone another step when a shout reached her from what felt like yards away. "Where the hell is she?"

Her heart stopped beating. She knew the voice was Atiernan's as surely as she knew her own—the rumbling, deep tones seemed to be a part of her, sinking into her skin.

"Where the hell is she?" he snarled again, the floor trembling beneath his heavy footsteps. Miranda could only imagine that he was pacing, roaming up and down the halls, searching for her.

Panicked, she ducked back into the room she'd just exited, closing the door silently.

"I haven't seen her," another voice chimed in. A voice she recognized to have the same, rasping tones as Atiernan—Benjamin. "Perhaps Peony knows?"

"She *doesn't*," Atiernan growled in reply. "Peony's the one who sent me looking for her in the first place. I just hope she isn't out by the perimeter…"

Peony? Why on earth would the mage send Atiernan after her? It was only when she pressed her ear against the door that she realized, for once, she was not the focus of the warrior's attention.

"Beth knows better," the second voice tried to reason. "She wouldn't dare go out of the—"

"She wouldn't dare do a lot of things before. None of us would. But now that *bitch* is here, everyone's on edge."

Ouch. Miranda had a sinking suspicion as to who the "bitch" was.

"We'll find her," his companion said. "If it is really the sentinels out there, they won't be able to get inside so quickly—not without help. She'll be fine."

"I hope you're right," Atiernan said grimly.

Miranda waited with her ear pressed so firmly to the door that it ached. They sounded close, close enough to smell her fear if she wasn't careful.

"Let's look again," Benjamin said finally. "You go left. I'll take the upper floor."

Damn, Miranda thought in horror. *Left* was the same direction as her cell.

Maybe she could sneak around the other end and slip inside before Atiernan noticed her?

There was only one way to find out.

She listened, heart straining against her ribcage, as the warriors' footsteps faded. Then, as carefully as she dared, she crept into the empty hall, praying to the gods that Atiernan, with his supernatural hearing and smell, couldn't sense her. Thankfully, the hall seemed to curve, hiding her from his view. If only she could move faster. If only her heart wasn't beating quite so rapidly, then—

Up ahead, a door opened, and Miranda did the only thing she could. As quickly as though the devil were on her heels, she ducked into the nearest room and pressed herself against the wall.

Nearby, she could hear the sound of soft footsteps heading in her direction, and frantically, she turned, finding a staircase at her feet.

It could have led anywhere, taking her deeper into the house, but she didn't have much of a choice. Blindly, she took the steps two at a time, practically sprinting. Her mind was a blinding rush of terror—a mantra of *hide, hide, hide —must escape Atiernan.*

She didn't even think before slipping from the alcove of the stairs and into a narrow hall, but like the one before it, the corridor was thankfully empty. It didn't seem to be too late or too early for foot traffic, meaning that the daemons were gathered somewhere else in the manor. Just how perilous of a situation were they in?

Very, if the fear she'd heard in Atiernan's voice was any indicator. He was worried, and—despite everything—that worried her in turn. Like it or not, she was under the man's protection in a sick sense of the word. If he fell, so did she...

"What are you doing here?"

Miranda bit her lip to keep from crying out as the voice came from behind her.

She turned, expecting to find a fully-grown daemon, threatening to drag her back to Atiernan. Instead, she came face to face with a figure barely taller than she was. It was the same girl from yesterday, with her long black hair divided neatly into two plaits.

"You're supposed to be in the dungeon," she said, placing a pale hand on her hip. Her wide brown eyes were narrowed into slits. "Atiernan said—"

"Oh, damn Atiernan!"

Miranda didn't know what the hell came over her, but she couldn't even bear to hear the man's name mentioned. It triggered something inside her—something hot and heavy that tingled at the ancient syllables.

She turned her back on the girl and marched in the opposite direction, trying to find the way to the dungeons.

"Hey!" Footsteps followed in her wake. "You're supposed to be—"

"What are *you* doing down here?" Miranda whirled on the girl, who took a step back. "Come to gawk at the captive witch? Considering the way everyone else around here treats me, you're either brave or stupid."

She didn't mean for the words to come out so harsh, but the girl's eyes darkened as she jutted her chin fiercely into the air. "Atiernan says that a good warrior always keeps an eye on their enemy."

Which she considered Miranda to be, if the way she was glaring at her was any indicator. Any other day, Miranda might have felt insulted—even the children here had something against her.

As it was, she was just too damn tired to care.

"I don't give a damn what you *or* Atiernan think of me—"

"Well, you should." The girl's dark eyes flashed, and to Miranda's horror, two tiny fangs descended to pierce her lower lip.

She shouldn't have been surprised. Atiernan had to keep humans here—if only to...feed. But they were most likely sequestered in another part of the manor. Only the daemons seemed to roam freely, and this girl, who appeared to be no older than a teenager, was one of them.

"The only reason you're still alive, witch, is because of him," the girl began indignantly. "The others want him to scry you. To get our answers from your mind—"

"What?" *Mind. Answers.* The words made Miranda's blood run cold. She had heard rumors of daemons who could pull secrets from the thoughts of others, but she had never thought...

"He told them he wouldn't." The girl's fangs flashed as she added, "I think he should."

Without a word, Miranda turned and headed down a random hallway. Damn the dungeons. If Atiernan considered her so evil, then he would have to lock her up himself.

"Wait!" She heard the girl rush after her. "Where are you going? You can't—"

"Beth."

The rumbling tone made both her and the daemon freeze in their tracks.

"L-Lord Atiernan." The girl blinked as the man in question rounded the corner. Suddenly, she stood straighter, fidgeting with the hem of her dress. "I was just…"

"Get to your mother, Beth. She's looking for you." Atiernan jerked his head in the stair's direction. Without another word, the girl darted off—but not without first giving Miranda a look that could only be described as…

Pitying.

Hell, even Atiernan's own people knew that being alone with the man was not a good sign. Miranda trembled, toying with the thought of running to her cell and shutting herself in—saving him the trouble of dragging her there. Even the dark wasn't half as intimidating as the daemon staring her down with those piercing eyes.

"What are you doing?" His tone was dangerously soft, and Miranda couldn't resist the urge to gulp. Her eyes darted to his upper lip, unintentionally searching for those fangs.

Thankfully, they were out of sight.

"I had to use the bathroom," she stammered, stumbling back until her body hit the wall.

The distance wasn't nearly far enough away from Atiernan as she wanted to be. The daemon loomed above her. She couldn't even bring herself to look at him head-on.

"The bathroom?" He sounded so skeptical, that Miranda wondered if the daemon was aware that normal humans relied on that typical bodily function.

"Yes," she snapped. Irritation overpowered her fear, and she started down the hall, hoping to outrun him. "I'm going back now—"

"Wait." Before she'd even gone a step, he caught her by the wrist. "There is a *bucket* in your cell, witch."

Miranda blanched at the suggestion, but those piercing eyes were anything but mocking.

"Well, that's an improvement to your hospitality," she said weakly. "Considering the slop I've been fed."

It wasn't the whole truth. While not exactly five-star cuisine, the simple soup and bread she'd been served hadn't exactly been prison portions.

Compared to what she usually ate, one might say she had no right to complain at all.

Atiernan just smiled, and the sight chilled her down to the bone. She'd made a mistake by provoking him.

"There are many ways I could 'feed' you, witch," he murmured.

She gulped. It wasn't the darkly mocking tone that had her shaking, or that cold smile. The subtle way he *said* those words had her trembling in fear, even before he turned down the hall, dragging her after him.

TEN

H e moved so quickly. It was a struggle to keep up with his long strides, and Miranda found herself panting by the time Atiernan finally hauled her into a spacious room with a vaulted ceiling and lit candles lining the walls.

A dining room?

A long table stood in the center, surrounded by high-backed wooden chairs and moving figures who seemed like servants at a glance. But even Miranda could tell that they were human.

"Lord Atiernan—" A woman with long blond hair approached them, holding a silver pitcher. "Dinner will not be served for a few hours."

"My apologies Aria," Atiernan said, surprising Miranda by the genuine kindness in his tone. Apparently, she was the one he reserved his disdain for. "But I would like to have my meal early—" Miranda shivered as his gaze cut in her direction. "My guest would like to sample something other than…slop."

Miranda turned crimson as the mortal's blue eyes took her in with one confused sweep. Rather than insulted, the woman just nodded. "Oh? Of course, sir."

She stood back to reveal several other women arranging silverware over the massive table. To Miranda's surprise, there seemed to be pale-skinned daemons mingled in amongst the humans, who all seemed clean and well-fed. Together, they froze, watching with awe as Atiernan dragged her inside.

With little more than a grunt, the daemon lord shoved her into a velvet-upholstered chair before taking the one beside her. He kept a grip on her arm, reminding her of a dog kept on a leash by a wary owner.

Aria, the mortal, was between them in an instant, pouring a dark liquid into a silver chalice that seemed to appear from nowhere—the work of two other servants who moved as silent as shadows.

Atiernan chuckled at her expense as she warily eyed the scarlet drink.

"It's wine," he said.

"Could be poisoned," she weakly replied. Regardless, she would rather drink her own blood than anything the daemon could offer. To prove as much, she pushed the chalice away with the back of her hand.

"Could be." Eyes flashing, Atiernan downed the contents of his chalice in one gulp, and a servant was there to take it before he could even finish wiping his mouth. "But make trouble, and you won't have to fear something as subtle as poison."

Miranda would have laughed if she wasn't too busy shaking. "I was looking for my cell."

"Hmm." His mouth formed a smile fit for the Devil himself. "I'm sure you were."

He tapped the surface of the table, and the next second, trays of food appeared as the servants rushed to follow his unspoken bidding.

Miranda couldn't help the fact that she stared. Maybe her stomach even grumbled once or twice in defiance. The daemon seemed to keep his home supplied with food fit for a king. Though it was "hours" before the main meal, as Aria had insisted, they were served freshly roasted duck and intricate dishes that Miranda hadn't seen grace her own table since…

Well, never. Witches didn't eat this grandly every damn night. This, she had a feeling, was nothing out of the norm for him. The man didn't bat an eyelash as he reached for a knife and cut himself a chunk of meat.

Miranda stared, oddly entranced as he brought the grisly morsel to his teeth and bit. The sight of those fangs made her shiver, almost as much as the fact that they bit into the meat without an ounce of hesitation. It wasn't raw. And it wasn't dripping blood, so why…

Fiery eyes caught hers, and she jerked her head away.

"Don't believe the stories you witches are told," Atiernan said. "We aren't savages, dining on roasted humans every night."

"But you drink blood," she pointed out. "Among other things."

Though he could eat food apparently—why the hell should she care? But it certainly contrasted with the narrative of dark, soulless monsters incapable of tolerating any ounce of human comfort that circled the coven.

Atiernan didn't seem to lack one bit of comfort. Against her will, Miranda's gaze was drawn back to him, and she watched as he chewed on a piece of bread. That wasn't the only thing odd about him. His warmth was an anomaly as far as Raeth daemons went.

Even being in the same room as Peony had made the air feel several degrees colder. More than that, his skin wasn't pale, but golden. Nearly tan.

Though his eyes were way too fierce for anyone to ever mistake him for a human.

She'd heard rumors before... Of a daemon who had committed so many atrocities—drunk so much fresh blood —that it changed him. Damned him, making the creature a twisted abomination of both daemon and mortal.

Could Atiernan possibly be that man? Watching him devour another serving of meat, Miranda couldn't tell.

"This is your chance to eat your fill, witch."

She jumped to realize that he'd been watching her almost as intently as she had been watching him.

"You'd be foolish to ignore it."

"Hmph." Deliberately, Miranda crossed her arms and thrust her chin into the air.

Without a word, Atiernan inclined his head, and a servant was there to take her plate away before she could even begin to change her mind.

"You think you're brave."

The observation threw her off. She shifted, turning to stare at one of the servants watching them from the shadows instead of him.

When she didn't answer, Atiernan continued as if she had.

"You think that denying *me* makes you brave. You're wrong, Miranda." Without even looking at her, he reached across the table for another piece of bread. "Denying me makes you foolish. I will treat you the way I treat any other enemy—"

"Oh?" A part of her trembled at that—how many other enemies did he ambush in the darkness and feed from? She could still feel the throbbing marks left by his teeth.

The shame alone made her shrivel inside, but she squared her jaw rather than show it.

"Whatever you give to me, you will receive," Atiernan said, his tone serious. "Treat me with hostility and distrust, and you will receive it. Respect me, and you shall receive respect. Betray me, and…"

Miranda could guess well enough what even he seemed too tactful to say.

"Rebuffing my attempts for peace doesn't score you any ounce of bravery."

What the hell did he know? Miranda was quite sure that denying him every damn chance she got was one hell of a way to uphold her honor. When she didn't answer, Atiernan chuckled again.

"Like I said, you get from me what I receive from you. You give me silence, then *silence* you shall have in return."

The tone was ominous, and his next words only proved how serious he was.

"From now on, you want to leave your cell? You call for me. You want to eat? You call for me. You want anything other than air and darkness? You call for *me*."

Each word sliced through Miranda like a knife.

"And if I don't?" She could barely bring herself to ask it.

Atiernan shrugged. With little effort, he snapped his fingers, and a servant appeared, holding a bowl of fruit from which he took a red apple.

"Then savor your last taste of freedom, witch," he said, tossing the fruit in front of her. "Hell, for all we know, this could be the last time you open that pretty mouth."

Miranda shuddered. Then, she stood, nearly tripping over a servant who had appeared to take away her chalice. Without a word, she stumbled from the room and turned blindly down the hall. A part of her was surprised that the daemon didn't grab her before she could so much as step over the threshold—but when she gathered the nerve to glance over her shoulder, she could see him looming a few paces behind.

She nearly ran the rest of the way, shaking by the time she finally found the steps leading to the dungeon and staggered inside her cell.

A second later, she flinched at the sound of the lock sliding home.

CHAPTER
ELEVEN

Miranda nearly cried with relief when her cell door creaked open the next morning. Whether Atiernan had stayed true to his word, or the daemon had been merely exercising a cruel streak, there had been no usual meal delivered to her that night. Besides the scuttling of rats, she had heard no one else wandering the long corridor outside her cell, either.

All of those insults were easy to endure.

But the darkness…

A few hours of freedom and already the stone chamber seemed as intimidating as it had that first night. Only the flicker of torchlight seen beneath the crack in the door kept her sane enough to focus. Not scream. Not panic. To avoid giving into base impulses and forsaking her vows as a witch. Gods above, she needed access to her natural magic. Good magic.

I am a Hazel witch, she insisted. Even the daemon appeared to respect her in that instance. While Atiernan wanted her to trade magic in return for freedom—he seemed to only have honest spells and potions in mind. Nothing more.

Nowhere near the cost she typically paid to be freed from the darkness...

Still, in the absence of torture, she suffered in another way. There was nothing to distract from the memories of Atiernan and the scrape of deliciously sharp fangs toying with sensitive flesh.

Suddenly, footsteps approached, piercing the quiet.

Thinking of the daemon, she bit her lip to trap any sound of relief as she lurched to her feet and waited. Maybe now she'd finally get some damn food? After sleeping on an empty stomach, she almost regretted sticking her nose up at the meal Atiernan had offered her. Almost.

When the door opened fully, Miranda didn't even have to glance up to know who stood on the other side of it—but she did anyway.

His eyes glowed a dangerous hue of amber, holding her captive for so long that the dungeon faded away for a moment. Blinking, she swayed on her feet as reality returned. Would he hurt her? Try once again to feed from her neck?

All he did was stare, his expression unreadable. He didn't even toss her his usual coarse greeting of "witch" before leaving her cell.

Traipsing in his shadow, Miranda was achingly aware of just how much of a toll several days of captivity had taken on her. She smelled. Her skin felt sticky with sweat, and her hair... Gods, she couldn't even think about that.

A part of her vainly hoped that the man was leading her to a bathroom, stocked with fresh clothes. In the end, she wasn't really surprised when he showed her to the small storeroom instead.

Peony was waiting for her. Like before, she practically sparkled with energy, but those gray eyes were subdued from behind the lenses of her glasses.

"An hour, Atiernan," she said. Without a word, the warrior turned and headed back down the hall.

Alone with the mage, Miranda found herself sorting herbs and labeling ingredients. Apparently, Peony had gotten her fill of potion crafting the other night, because she barely glanced up from a pile of dusty scrolls while Miranda worked. The silence was so suffocating that it was nearly a relief when Peony finally told her that their time was done for the day.

"Tell him you did good," the mage said without looking up from her reading. "I want you again tomorrow."

As she stumbled from the doorway, Miranda wondered just how in the hell she was going to find Atiernan, let alone tell him anything. The moment her foot crossed the threshold, however, she could sense him there as oppressive as a raincloud.

Once again, he didn't say a word to her—he didn't even acknowledge her presence at all. Miranda half-expected him to take her back to the dungeons and trap her inside her cell, but instead…

He led her to the end of the hall and stopped near a doorway. Heart pounding, she peeked inside the room beyond and nearly gasped out loud.

It was a bathroom. Achingly aware of what Beth said the other day, she wondered if the bastard had—literally—read her mind. Too damn desperate to care, she stumbled inside anyway, wrestling the door shut behind her.

The filthy clothing couldn't come off her fast enough, and when the hot water finally touched her body, she fought to smother a sigh of relief. As a captive, she should have washed quickly, unwilling to dwell in the comforts bestowed by an enemy. Two seconds into her soak and she gave in. Damn the circumstances. It felt good to wipe the grime from her skin.

She could almost forget where she was… If it wasn't for the constant prickle along the side of her throat.

But the daemon's odd display of kindness hadn't come without a catch, she realized once she finally climbed from the tub, dripping wet.

The only clothes in sight—waiting, neatly folded on the counter—were a gaudy shade of pink and comically small. Like something meant for a child.

He'd given her children's clothing.

A glance at the floor revealed her brown dress was missing.

The sad part was, before she even had the chance to feel indignant, she realized that the garment was roughly the same size she wore anyway. The only difference was that the pink dress, sporting a smattering of bright red hearts, was not her usual modest attire—neither was the pair of pink cotton panties she found alongside it.

At least they were *something*. Recalling her old, crumpled dress—covered in nearly a week of filth—she couldn't even bring herself to feel angry.

Just a faint bit of shame as she realized the sleeves were too short, exposing her forearms. No matter. It wasn't like the beasts would blanch at her scars, and she would never explain their origins.

When she finally tiptoed back into the hall, Atiernan waited for her.

He stared, amber eyes boldly taking her in. Miranda half expected him to laugh at her standing there, dripping wet in a child's dress, but...

She couldn't shake the feeling that he was waiting for something. A thank you?

Whatever it was, all he got from her was the sound of her jaw clenching shut as she turned to stare in the opposite direction.

He sighed—the sound nearly a growl—and a second later, his heavy footsteps retreated down the hall, and she followed him without thinking. As they passed an open window, she could tell that the sun had already begun to set, sinking behind a swath of trees.

Just how long had he kept her in her cell?

Many of the daemons were still awake, wandering the halls. Seeing her cowering behind their leader, they frowned. A few tried to make eye contact with him—but Atiernan just kept moving, head held high, and no one dared to question him out loud.

Not even Miranda.

Maintaining their unspoken silent contest, she followed behind as he entered a wide-open room where a desk stood at the center. As if waiting for him, several daemons had already gathered in the corners, watching as Atiernan crossed the room with her in tow.

The moment the daemon lord took a seat behind the desk, those before him formed an orderly line. The first man— after sparing a wary glance in her direction—began to spout off a list of supplies at Atiernan's bidding.

After the leader gave a curt response, another figure stepped forward to voice a similar statement.

The whole set-up reminded Miranda of a king's court. Sitting in his high-backed chair, Atiernan certainly looked regal enough to be one. A part of her couldn't help but wonder if she had made a mistake by following him.

Judging from the wary glances his people sent her way, this wasn't the type of event that an enemy should be privileged to. They spoke about food stores, and the perimeter of the manor—sensitive information that Miranda knew she could have easily used to her advantage if she ever returned to her coven.

But, after seeing the man in action over the past few days, she had to admit that Atiernan wasn't stupid. While a brute, he must have known damn well what having her present at this meeting meant—and so did she.

She might as well drink in all the information to her heart's content, because she wouldn't be leaving this manor with a shred of knowledge still in her head. If he allowed her to leave alive...

Suddenly dizzy, she stumbled into a corner and collapsed onto a stool—unnoticed by the daemons who continued to file before Atiernan, one by one, presenting their various reports or voicing a complaint.

After a while, even that got monotonous. Ignoring the way her stomach growled, Miranda found herself drifting off, her mind filled with visions of blood...

TWELVE

After more than several thousand years of life, Atiernan could readily admit his faults—it had been a mistake to give her Beth's clothes. What had been intended as a cruel joke backfired when he saw just how well Miranda fit the bright pink cotton. The hem rode just a little too high over her creamy thighs, and the curved neckline only exposed the red marks left by his fangs.

Damn. Bethaem would never be able to wear that dress again—not that she ever had. He made sure to only borrow the girlish items her father bought the girl in a futile attempt to counteract what he saw as the "morbid effects" of her being raised part daemon.

Still, the way Miranda filled out the ridiculous garment was downright unholy. And despite himself… Atiernan couldn't ignore the painful tightening of the front of his slacks. He could barely keep his mind on the task at hand. Not with her scent heavy on the air, and her warm and waiting so close.

Would she taste any different, cleaned and dripping wet from her bath?

He hated himself for thinking the thought. Hated himself more for the way his fangs elongated, teasing the inside of his mouth in anticipation. He barely heard what was being said as Benjamin approached, a smirking Sanna in tow.

"The perimeter is all clear, my lord," the daemon said, his fangs flashing as he caught sight of Miranda in the corner. "But are you sure it is wise to have *her* outside the dungeon?"

Atiernan turned to see that she had fallen asleep, resting her head against the wall. Her chest rose and fell in a slow, easy rhythm that had him picturing her pulse, even as his ears strained to hear it. Something steady enough to dance to. *Thump...thump...thump.*

"Lord Atiernan?"

"G-Good," he stammered, rising to his feet. He shook his head firmly to clear it and gestured to those gathered in the room with a wave of his hand. "Thank you. That is enough for the day. Back to your duties."

They left, leaving no one there to witness as Atiernan turned to the witch, nostrils flaring as he tasted her scent on the air.

It was strange to find she had let her guard down. Sleeping, she didn't seem like quite the haughty bitch she was when awake. He could almost pretend that she wasn't that woman

—just admire the sleeping figure who seemed eerily beautiful as a ray of moonlight cut across that pale skin, illuminating the high cheekbones.

But even asleep, she was far from relaxed. Inadvertently hostile, she had her arms crossed tightly over her chest, hair brushing her shoulders like silk. For some reason, Atiernan felt a strange impulse to run his fingers through those strands. See what they felt like. Thankfully, a burst of common sense crushed the urge before it could take root.

Instead, he inspected her wrists, noting that the binding charm was still intact. That wasn't all—her skin wasn't as flawless as he first thought. Odd. Witches were typically more self-conscious than most, preferring to project an aura of physical and moral purity. He'd never seen one sport so much as a scratch, and certainly not to this extent. Scars riddled nearly every inch of Miranda's exposed forearms. They were ugly—thickened, silvery flesh that looked rough to the touch.

A grunt of alarm ripped from him as he advanced a step without thinking. What wounds could have caused such injuries? Nothing accidental. This was...torture?

Enough. He hissed and refocused on the task at hand—dealing with the sentinel threat, the only reason this woman remained in his presence. Her personal history meant nothing to him, intriguing as it seemed to be.

"Witch." His voice echoed, making her jump and nearly fall off the stool.

She recovered quickly and staggered to her feet, forcing her trembling hands down by her sides. "Y-Yes?"

Did she even realize that this was the first time he had spoken to her that night? He fully intended to maintain the wall of silence indefinitely, but...

Here, alone in this room with her, he couldn't help himself. His eyes traveled directly to her throat, watching the blue line of a vein play underneath the white skin. Then lower, to the delicate mounds straining the pink material.

His palm twitched, remembering the feel of one delicate breast. How her pulse had played like a lullaby through her skin. He could smell her from here. That intoxicating scent engulfed him, and he took another step forward before he could help it. She fell back, sucking in a breath. The motion brought Atiernan's attention to the heartbeat pounding out a symphony of fear within her chest.

Deliberately, he took another step. And then another... unable to help the way the fear in her eyes resonated with some deep-seated part of him that wanted to fully experience that terror. One hundred percent. Completely.

Only to gradually switch it over to pleasure until she couldn't possibly stand anymore.

"Stay...stay back."

Atiernan blinked, shocked to find himself only a short distance from her. "What's wrong?" he asked, alarmed by the guttural tone of his voice. "Afraid?"

Her chin jutted proudly into the air even as her throat quivered. "Never! You need to do far more than dress me in frills to scare me, daemon."

She had a point. He'd merely been toying with her until now—but with every passing second, the sentinels inched closer. Would he really let that threat descend without at least pushing the witch to help? *Demanding* she do so. Damn Peony and her methods.

There were other ways to coerce the witch's help, whether she wanted to give it or not.

"You are right," he agreed. "I should do far more."

"Then what are you waiting for?" Her brown eyes were fierce, proudly boring into his, and Atiernan couldn't help himself. He grabbed her by the shoulder and surged the two steps necessary to pin her between his body and the wall.

No more games—if she wanted to play the role of defiant captive, this was a fitting position. Crushed against him, arousing his bloodlust and…another, just as volatile, lust.

The delicious friction had him growling low in the base of his throat. Suddenly, he was aware of every part of him her body touched—the firm nipples stabbing through the cotton of his shirt. The narrow waist. Her hot breath on his skin.

And he only wanted to experience more.

"How about now?" He reached out to snag a lock of dark hair and pulled until she winced. The motion forced her to meet his gaze, but he was annoyed to find that she didn't hesitate to.

"How about *now*, witch?" he asked, his voice thick. "Are you afraid?"

She needed to be.

Because *he* was. She appealed to a part of him he'd spent millennia suppressing. Who knew what he might be capable of should those impulses return?

But, in the name of saving his people, did he have any right to be restrained?

The answer was simple—no.

One witch wasn't worth the lives of those in his pack and never would be.

THIRTEEN

Uh-oh. The childish statement flitted across her mind before Miranda could suppress it. Sometime during that quick conversation, she'd said the wrong thing. Trapped against Atiernan's bulk, she couldn't remember what that might have been. She couldn't breathe. Her nostrils flared on a desperate quest for air to no avail. Her lungs burned, and every inch of her seared with invisible fire.

Though, to be fair, much of it had nothing at all to do with lack of oxygen.

The daemon was everywhere. Above and below. Blocking her in from every side. Oppressive, and at the same time, so deliciously *unbearable* she couldn't stand it.

The old crones preached of corruption and the horrors awaiting young witches outside the coven's woods. Tales of dangerous men and bloodthirsty daemons.

None mentioned the thrill of being the victim of such attention. Perhaps the way her heart lurched was merely a side effect of her cursed blood. Yet more proof that she was tainted—reacting to a daemon with anything but abject disgust.

"P-Please," she croaked, hating herself for displaying any sign of weakness in front of him. "Let me go—"

"No." Atiernan turned, dragging her after him to the center of the room where that desk waited. "Remember?" His tone had her gulping, even as he wrenched her around to face him. "My bargain, witch?"

Thinking that he meant the one dealing with Peony, she stammered out a pathetic, "Yes," only to have the man laugh in her face.

"No, not that one." He captured her chin in his palm before she could blink. With lethal softness, his thumb traced her upper lip as if to mimic the path of nibbling fangs.

Something was wrong.

The look in those amber eyes was different...strange. Miranda barely recognized the daemon. Suddenly, he seemed taller, and those canines peeking from his upper lip looked a little sharper than before. Feral. Even his skin glowed, and Miranda felt every inch of her tingle with the awareness of a predator.

"I meant the one after," he said, voice dark with meaning.

It took her a second, but once she did finally remember, her eyes went wide. *You want anything other than air and dark-*

ness? You call for me."

"'You can't be serious…'"

"Oh yes, I am." His smile expanded, revealing the two sharp canines glistening from either corner. "Only now, I think I may rearrange my terms. Instead of receiving what you give, from now on, I will just *take* what I want from you—"

He leaned in and braced a firm hand on either side of her. His next words fanned her throat in a fiery whisper. "You want me to stop, Miranda?"

He snatched the hem of her dress and toyed with it. She didn't dare look down, tracking his movements from the corner of her eye instead. He twisted the pink fabric between his fingers. Then tugged. A tiny ripping sound was all she heard next as he promptly tore it, plunging a thumb through the cotton to brush her skin.

"You *beg*."

The threat would have been comical if it wasn't for the look in his eyes. That teasing, taunting, *burning* look that warned her thoroughly—this was no game.

"I-I don't beg," Miranda forced herself to croak, but the words sounded hollow to her own ears. She was already trembling with fear. As if well aware of that fact, Atiernan released her dress to cup her thigh. A gasp escaped her. Each firm finger burned, imprinting into her flesh.

"Oh?" He chuckled, and Miranda knew that the sound would haunt her nightmares for eternity. "I wonder…"

She had no warning. Absolutely nothing to alert her to his intentions before she found herself lying back against the desk's wooden surface with him looming above. Before she could react, his fingers danced the length of her thigh, slowly moving inward. Higher...

Somehow, she found the strength to push him off and lurch upright. "Let me go, you bastard—"

"I said beg," Atiernan countered, shoving her back down.

Stars danced before her eyes though he hardly used any force. Maybe the sensation had something to do with the ache she could feel building in the pit of her stomach, matching the tempo of those searching fingers as they deliberately prodded her inner thigh?

"Let's put it to the test." His fangs flashed, and the skin of her neck prickled in grim anticipation. "You want me to stop? *Beg* me to."

Was he insane? Had the man jumped off some hidden ledge to madness? Whatever the reason, the carefully controlled Lord of Daemons had transformed into a monster.

"Atiernan..." She tried to keep her tone level. Obviously, he wanted to scare her. "L-Let me go—"

He shook his head. "That doesn't sound like a plea to me." His eyes were molten orbs of fire searing her down to the bone. "I have treated you with all the respect you deserve, but if you want to be a prisoner?" He shrugged and moved his hand from her leg...to her throat.

"I have no problem treating you like one."

Atiernan's gone, a part of her whispered with a cold sense of finality that had her shaking. *This isn't him—it's someone else.*

Someone who didn't seem to care that he had torn a hole through the bottom of her borrowed children's dress. That his fingers—coarse and calloused from what she guessed was years of fighting—were currently tracing foreign patterns into her skin.

His hand encased her throat, leaving only enough room to breathe.

Barely.

The slight pressure had her lightheaded. Dizzy, she tried to push him off. For all the effort she made, the man might have been formed of *concrete* rather than flesh.

He was immovable. Stone. He watched her attempts with a frown, staring down at her hands as if they were little more than flies.

Then...

All at once, he let her go.

Dazed, Miranda clung to the desk for balance, trying to catch her breath. Trying to catch... *Something.* Her heart, maybe? It seemed ready to burst through her chest and dart across the room in a way she felt too weak to.

"W-what the hell is wrong with you?" she stammered at Atiernan's back as he turned away.

If she wasn't mistaken...his words reached her on a sigh, "I don't know."

CHAPTER
FOURTEEN

She didn't know how long she cowered in the study after the daemon finally left. All night? It had to be close to morning when a far-off sound finally penetrated the walls, but it was too shrill to be voices. A siren?

"Everyone to the inner chamber *now*—something is wrong," an unfamiliar voice rang out.

"Sentinels?" came a woman's soft cry. "Not now...by the gods, not now."

"Come on, we should take shelter."

By the time Miranda finally stood and crept into the hall, it was dead silent with no one in view. She should have felt relieved, but dread flooded her belly instead. Something big was going on—big enough to terrify a house full of daemons.

Could it be the sentinels? For the first time since hearing about the wretched creatures, she truly felt afraid. The others had mentioned an inner chamber, but she had no clue where it might be. Her only hope was to return to her cell and lock herself inside.

She took a few hesitant steps, picking a direction at random. It wasn't long before she realized navigating this manor was easier said than done. She couldn't remember which route Atiernan had taken to bring her here.

Wandering aimlessly, she finally found a staircase, but rather than the dungeon, it led to a massive kitchen brimming with the smells of fresh food. Like the rest of the house, it was utterly empty, with no one around to stir the pots of steaming food or cut the vegetables left to wilt on the counters. Though her stomach grumbled, Miranda didn't dare steal a bite to eat. Instead, the ominous dread welling within her grew, spurring her on.

For once, the enclosed darkness of the dungeons seemed safer than out in the open. If only she could remember just how to get there. As the hallway curved, she turned, intending to go back the way she'd come, when a noise from the darkness made her jump.

A quiet rustling, so soft it could have been a trick of her senses. Until a growl all but shattered that naïve theory.

It wasn't the sound of the average dog. No… There were words mingled within the coarse notes. "I smell the warrior…he is near."

The voice did not belong to Atiernan—or any of his men. Nothing human and nothing daemon. It was a low, deep purr like that of an animal attempting to use mortal language.

More bluntly—it was the voice of pure, unfiltered evil, and Miranda went pale in the face of it. Before she could think to run, the rustling sounds intensified into the eerie scrape like that of claws raking over tiled floors.

Good gods, she could *smell* it. A powerful, animalistic stench that made her stomach roil. Fear drenched her in cool sweat, nothing like the terror that gripped her in the face of Atiernan.

She held her breath and pressed her back to the wall, hoping beyond hope that the creature didn't catch her scent...

"He is near," that fearsome voice growled once more. "*Near*...I can smell it."

Atiernan? Whoever it hunted for, it wouldn't be long before the creature fell upon her first. The rustling sound grew louder, drawing her notice to a doorway across from the kitchens.

A monstrous shadow blocked the light, leaving only a void of darkness from which she could see nothing.

Nothing but a pair of ruby red eyes.

Run! She whirled on her heel and raced through the nearest doorway. There wasn't time for stealth. She ran blindly, following the curve of the hall until it opened into a massive drawing room.

It was there that her foot caught on a rut in the floor, sending her sprawling. She tried to stand, but a sharp noise made her turn just as a monstrous thud shattered the quiet, followed by the hiss of scraping claws.

Gods, she thought frantically, eyes scanning the room for a way out. For once, she wished that someone else was around—Atiernan. Anyone.

"*Him*," the voice crooned, snapping her back to the frightful reality. Whatever the creature was, it had gained on her already. "The hunter…he is near."

Down the hall, a pair of blood-red eyes seemed to glimmer through the shadows as the beast advanced, moving far more quickly, and with more grace, than its size bellied. There was almost a beauty in the terribleness of it.

It seemed to stretch the tight walls of the hall, ripping pictures, and smashing lights as it crawled its way after her. The closer it came, the more the bright light of the great room exposed its body in terrifying detail.

It was pale, covered in milk-white flesh that seemed nearly translucent. Moving in a halting gait, it was hunched on all fours, with a small, triangular head from which jutted two rows of massive, glistening canines.

At the sight of her, the creature howled, its mouth opening to reveal the gnarled teeth awaiting within.

"Him," it growled gleefully, advancing on thick, oddly bent legs that ended in four sharp claws. With every inch it gained, they pierced the floor, leaving jagged lines behind.

Before Miranda could flinch, it was closer. With a chilling hiss, its mouth parted near her splayed feet, and she braced for it to bite.

"The hunter..." it murmured instead, inhaling her scent through slit-like nostrils.

Miranda could only stare. In the pit of her soul, she knew just what it had smelled.

"Atiernan."

Somehow, the sound of the warrior's name gave her the strength to lurch forward on her hands and knees. Her dress bunched up around her legs, hampering her movements. She almost considered tearing it off, but...

A deep voice bellowed out, clearing her mind of everything but hope. "Hey!"

Her heart soared as a tall figure raced into view. She couldn't stop a single name from escaping her lips, "Atiernan..."

But no. This man was different, with long dark hair instead of red. Rather than all black, he wore gray sweatpants and a white T-shirt riddled with streaks of mud as if he ventured through a forest on foot. In one hand, he brandished a blade that sparkled wickedly in the glow of lamplight.

"Atiernan!" the creature bellowed, and Miranda had only the hiss of parting air as a warning before pain sliced through her left leg. She collapsed, moaning in agony as the creature lurched past her.

There wasn't time to wallow in shock. Teeth gritted, she rolled over and clawed her way forward, dragging her legs behind her.

Not far away, an eerie shriek pierced the air, and she looked over, finding that the dark-haired stranger had sliced the beast across its chest.

Their eyes met, and Miranda swore she saw his lips move, forming a single word. She couldn't hear him clearly, but his expression was insistent. "Move!"

He didn't need to tell her twice, and—armed or not—she sensed that he alone couldn't take on such a beast unscathed. Whipping her head toward the hall, Miranda threw herself forward. *Atiernan,* she thought frantically as the monster bellowed his name again. If only the warrior did come. If only...

The sound of rapid footsteps seemed to answer her prayers, and she looked up, vision blurring as another figure raced in from the hall. But, as the light washed over her rescuer, her hopes faded and died with the rise of a new fear.

"Run," she shrieked at the young daemon girl, who stood frozen in horror of what she'd walked in on. Miranda recognized her—the teenager who sometimes lurked outside Peony's storeroom.

"Run!" she shouted again, willing the girl to listen. "Run! Go!"

She made the mistake of looking back to find the sentinel crouched nearby—but no one else. The dark-haired man had vanished, leaving no one to protect them.

Protect her.

"Run!" Whirling back to the girl, Miranda lurched to her feet, wincing at the pain.

It was already too late. With a howl of bloodlust, the creature moved, and Miranda did the only thing she could.

She pivoted, putting herself directly into the path of the careening monster.

It hit her like a sledgehammer blow, rattling her bones—breaking some of them—and knocking the breath from her chest as all its heavy, crushing weight fell upon *her* instead of the daemon girl.

She could only will the child to run, fast and hard, while she still could, as the beast's fangs descended into her neck in a flash of brutalizing pain. Her last clear thought was that it was nothing like when Atiernan had bitten her.

There was no delicious heat or sensual burn. The creature was larger—unbelievably stronger—and its fangs didn't just sink deep but *tear* and *rip* as a snake-like mouth gulped greedily at her blood…

From far away, Miranda heard herself scream.

A cry cut far too short in a gurgle of blood.

FIFTEEN

A tiernan heard the scream, two stories above near the inner chamber where most of the pack took shelter, secured. Instantly, he took off down the hall without waiting for backup.

Only a handful of people had yet to arrive. One absence, in particular, made his heart lurch as he attempted to picture the scream's owner. *No,* he thought desperately. *Not Beth. Gods no, not Beth...*

He didn't think, just moved, allowing his senses to lead him down the stairs and through the hall that led to the great room where his pack sometimes held meetings. On those days, it would be packed full of people, bursting with chatter and voices.

Now, it brimmed with blood—the smell so potent his vision turned red as the predator within him stirred, called forth by its magnetic pull. A brilliant scarlet, the liquid painted the floors of the foyer, and smeared the walls in a violent spray.

At the center of it all lay a motionless body he didn't have the heart to recognize. Above it crouched a sentinel feeding ravenously with grunting, growling sounds that made his stomach clench in disgust.

Before despair could take root, he caught sight of a familiar figure lurking just beyond the predator's reach—Beth, standing pale as a sheet in the corner. There wasn't time for relief. With a shout, Atiernan reached for her and shoved her toward the hall.

"Run!"

Alone, he faced the grim scene playing out before him. Without fear for Beth clouding his mind, he didn't recognize the figure beneath the sentinel. Their face was turned from him, the beast's massive head obscuring it as it fed messily from a torn shoulder.

The sounds…the smell.

It made him want to retch. But then, his nostrils flared, picking up the sweet tinge to the scent that he had missed before.

Eyes wide, he took in the dark hair spilling across the floor, the pale legs soaked in blood, and the torn pink dress. The sentinel had Miranda…

He didn't plan—just moved. Lightning quick, he threw himself on the creature with a howl more fitting of a wolf than a man. He gripped the monster's thick neck and dragged it free, throwing its massive body across the room.

It growled, blood flying from its bared fangs as it scrambled to its feet, rushing at him with a powerful surge of its hind legs.

Atiernan was ready for it and rammed a fist into the creature's side. Bones crunched in a spray of blood as the beast's pained howl fed the darkest impulses he normally kept at bay.

Yes, roared the warrior within him, relishing the scent of blood and the heat of battle.

Yes…

He bared his fangs, snarling—an animalistic, primal sound. After years of reining in his true side…this was what he was…

A bloodthirsty monster who longed only to kill. Never could he be anything else…

"Ugh."

The sound tore him from his bloodlust like a slap. He turned to Miranda's ravaged body, shocked as a pale hand twitched. She was still alive.

"Miranda—"

His words ended on a pained hiss as agony ripped through the meat of his thigh. He looked down to find the beast latched onto his leg, fangs sinking deep.

Atiernan lunged, gripping the monster's thick throat as shouts sounded nearby—his men, finally having heard the commotion.

Not that he needed the help.

Eyes ablaze with murderous lust, he tightened his grip and twisted, breaking the beast's neck. He tossed the carcass aside, already crouching beside Miranda's body, searching for a pulse.

He doubted he'd find one. Everything from her shoulder to her throat was a mass of bloodied, gaping flesh. The muscles were torn, arteries ripped, and blood rushed hot and wet to coat her skin. So much blood...

The moan he'd heard had to be her death knell—the last sound her sweet mouth would ever make. It was idiotic to hope for more, but Atiernan felt himself shrugging logic aside as he slipped the witch into his arms and stood.

His bitten leg throbbed—but the pain was nothing. He'd felt worse, and probably would experience worse throughout his lifetime.

If only the damn witch would stop bleeding! Her rich scent flooded his senses, making it hard to think...

"Atiernan!" someone shouted as a rush of bodies tore into the foyer. "Are you alright?"

"He's bleeding!"

One of his men approached and placed a hand on his shoulder, but Atiernan brushed them off. He only paused to nod toward the sentinel—it needed to be taken out and preferably burned before the other sentinels caught wind of it.

Then, he moved, pushing through the crowd, dripping blood, both his and Miranda's, as he headed almost blindly down the nearest hall.

It wasn't until a familiar voice reached his ears that he realized where he'd gone.

"Atiernan!" Peony cried from the doorway of her storeroom. "What the hell happened?"

No time, Atiernan thought frantically. He didn't even know if he formed the words at all. The darkness of the hall seemed to suffocate him as he stumbled forward, Miranda still in his arms.

Good gods…what was he going to do with her?

He couldn't hold her this way for long…not when her smell threatened to drive him mad. Not…

Not when he could scarcely fight down the predator awakened by his brush with the sentinel who urged him to bend his head and take from her what the monster had.

Damn. It was getting harder to resist with her fucking smell clogging his nose—her blood all over his hands.

Over *all* of him.

Even the pain in his leg used the battle in his mind to intensify until he could feel every drop of the creature's venom seeping through his veins. He would need treatment soon—

he knew that. They had an antidote—somewhere. He would need to ask Peony. He would need to...

Gods, what he really needed to do was heal the woman in his arms. Heal her fast...heal her now.

Because, if he didn't, he'd destroy her himself.

"Atiernan!"

He lifted his head, focusing on the slight figure rushing toward him. He knew that she could tell just how close he was to losing control. Agonized hunger roared in his veins, and his fangs began to throb in agreement, desiring the fresh blood they'd been denied for so long.

No!

With a growl, he forced his fangs to retract and presented Miranda's body.

"Let her go," Peony encouraged. "I will help her. Just let her go—"

No. He shook his head. No...

His throat worked to swallow, his vision threatening to turn red. She was *his.*

"Atiernan," Peony snapped. "Come here. Bring her to me. Follow the sound of my voice. Come."

He somehow managed to obey. Taking wide strides, he set Miranda down on the floor as gently as possible with his fingers shaking like mad. Torn, he turned to gaze into the calm, soft eyes of Peony. While her expression was soothing, her hands were held open at her sides, ready to fend him off in case he decided to strike.

The woman knew well what the sight of so much blood could do to a man like him. Gods, he was so close to breaking...so close.

He made an agonized sound in the back of his throat, fighting the urge to rip his gaze back to the witch. Peony had enough sense to move forward to slap him hard across the side of his cheek before he could move.

Pain made the rage flare—but only for a second before logic was able to rise and fully take hold.

"You are *not* that man," he heard Peony say sharply. "Be the one I raised you to be—*Now* Atiernan!"

And just like that, the predator's hold over him was broken.

"I'm... I'm okay." He breathed deep, shoulders heaving. Finally, his vision began to clear, and he could think straight.

"Leave the witch to me," the mage said, gripping the curve of his chin. "You tend to your men. *Leave this to me.*"

Atiernan nodded, barely finding the strength to resist the childish urge to collapse into the woman's arms like he had all those years ago amid the bloodiest war known to man.

In the end, it was a desire he didn't have the energy to fight.

His arms went around her, trapping her close, and Peony allowed herself to be hugged while running her fingers through his hair as one might soothe a young boy.

"You're alright," she murmured. "It will take more than this to affect you. *Much* more than this."

Atiernan nodded into the crook of her shoulder, hoping to the gods that she was right. It made him tremble to think he'd come so close—so close, to losing everything he'd worked so hard to maintain.

At this moment, he didn't even care whether he, or even Miranda, lived or died. He only needed to sleep, to sink into the dark warmth of dreams and erase this nightmare.

"You will," Peony murmured, reading his mind through her touch. "You *will* rest, Atiernan. But, first, I need you to stand. And take this—" She rushed into her storeroom. A heartbeat later, she returned with a small vial of brown liquid he recognized—antidote to sentinel venom. As he downed the substance, she met his gaze squarely. "Tend your men. *They* need you. We need you."

Yes. She was right.

With a nod, he pulled away, pushing past her into the open hall. The commotion wafting from below was catastrophic —he would need to work to contain this now, before panic spread and all hell broke loose.

At the doorway, he paused for one last look at the woman he'd nearly lost everything to save.

And then he left.

CHAPTER
SIXTEEN

Though she didn't like to think of it, Peony had lived to see thousands of years, if she felt the urge to take the time and count them. Her immortality was something she was not proud of, nor ashamed of.

She was what she was—a creature unbound by mortal constraints such as death.

At times she felt like a fire cursed to burn for eternity—unnatural, terrible, but still there. She had lived, and she would keep living until the gods felt the need to finally take this life from her.

But, of all the horror she'd witnessed, if she could erase the sight of Atiernan so close to becoming the monster he once was from her mind, she would.

The man was more like a son to her than a leader—they'd been through so much. He was strong, but at his core, he was still weak to the things that tempted him.

He was still a daemon.

And by the gods, Peony had never seen him so undone by a woman. Ever. Except, of course, Liva.

After her betrayal, Peony had sworn a vow never to be caught off guard by treachery again. While Miranda seemed far less ambitious than her counterpart, Peony would trust her only until she had a reason not to.

If only she could kill the witch now—despite her knowledge and magic. If she could erase the temptation that had brought Atiernan so close to losing control...

If she thought the witch's death would make a difference, Peony wouldn't hesitate to let her die.

No good would come out of Atiernan falling for her, and fall for her he was, even if the man himself didn't realize it yet. There was no other way the woman's blood could have affected him the way it did. If the fever was there in his soul, tempting him—trapping him—then he must have tasted the witch.

It was already too late. Atiernan would be bound to this woman, whether he liked it or not. It was up to her to make sure that the witch didn't come in harm's way again.

Peony knew in her gut that if she did, the man she loved like her own son, would never be the same again.

She'd already lost Conar...

She couldn't lose him too.

"Enough pitying," she hissed, snapping to her senses.

Shoulders back, head held high with determination, she turned to the fallen woman and felt for a pulse.

It was there. Faint and lazy, but palpable.

Peony didn't want to think about how she was still alive. All she knew was that sentinel bites could be deadly—her wound would need to be cleaned and properly dressed before she could ever begin to heal.

But she would.

Peony would see to it personally.

SEVENTEEN

The first thing Atiernan saw to the moment he returned downstairs was that the sentinel's body be taken out and burned.

It was a grim ceremony. With no words, no flourish, he, Benjamin, and two others worked to drag the beast's massive body out into the yard, far enough away from the house so that nothing of meaning could catch a spark and burn.

"We believe it came in through the door leading to the kitchen gardens," Ben said. "There were no signs of forced entry. You know what that means."

Damn. "Someone let it in," Atiernan said.

"And I'm sure we can guess who that might have been," his soldier replied.

Atiernan shrugged him off. "For now, let's destroy the damn thing."

Glaring at the body, Ben pulled a lighter from his pocket, flicked it open, and let it fall, alighting the creature in orange flames.

They stood there just long enough to make sure the monster was truly dead. Then, one by one, they returned silently to the house, going their separate ways to tend to the many pressing concerns spewing from everyone's mouths.

How had the sentinel gotten in? The answer was obvious, though Atiernan didn't want to admit it.

It had been *let* in—someone inside had opened the door.

By the gods…what if it had found the children?

As far as suspects went, only one name was at the forefront of everyone's lips.

"The witch," someone hissed as he walked past. Unintentionally, he wound up following the smeared path of blood leading into the great room. There, Beth was shaking, tears running down her chin as one of the women tried their hardest to comfort her.

He hadn't told Peony how close to danger the girl had come, he realized. Couldn't tell her, not until he made sure the girl was okay.

Ignoring the heated whispers of the others, he pushed his way toward her, and brushed her shoulder.

"Are you alright?" He hated how pained he sounded, how tormented.

Not counting Miranda, none of his people had been hurt, and his wounds, with the aid of Peony's antidote, had already healed. Despite a horrendous breach, he should have been relieved. Should have been angry at whoever had dared to put his people in danger.

As it was, he felt sick to his stomach, able to think only of blood.

Her blood.

"I'm fine," he heard Beth mutter weakly, though she didn't look fine. Her brown eyes were wide, and she trembled head to toe.

"I'm fine," she repeated, almost breathless. "Fine…"

Then all at once, she broke. "Oh gods, it bit her!" She wailed wordlessly, wrapping her arms around her chest like a child. "It bit her…It bit…"

"You're alright," Atiernan told her fiercely, engulfing her in his arms.

He could only thank the gods she hadn't been hurt. Peony had already lost Conar—as strong as the mage was, Atiernan didn't think she could survive losing Bethaem, too.

"You're alright," he repeated, pressing his mouth to the girl's scalp. "I'm here…It's alright."

"Oh Gods…she's dead," Beth sobbed, convulsing against his chest. "She's dead. She's dead."

"No, she's not," Atiernan said quietly. "She's alive."

Miranda would live. Though he wasn't sure if that was a good thing.

At his words, the woman rubbing Beth's back turned away, but not before he saw the mistrust in her eyes.

Ben wasn't the only one who suspected the witch of the unthinkable.

Gods, did she really hate them all so much that she would sacrifice herself just to see him burn? Had she done it on purpose? Opened the door to the sentinel, knowing she would die?

Was she truly so spiteful?

He didn't even have to see the accusing faces of his men to know the answer. Even so, he couldn't ignore the part of him that angrily railed against the suggestion. Miranda may have been proud, haughty, and stubborn, but she wasn't mad.

She wouldn't sacrifice her life just to see him fall. He was sure of it.

"You know what you need to do," Ben's voice came accusingly from over his shoulder.

Tiredly, Atiernan turned to face the warrior head-on. Behind him, stood three other men in silent solidarity.

"You know who did this," Ben snarled. "You *know* who is responsible."

There were murmurs of agreement. Having come so close to death, everyone was on edge, and Atiernan realized that he was not the only one hungry for blood.

If Miranda was responsible, he thought darkly…

She would pay. He would string her up himself.

But he *had* to be sure.

"You know what you have to do, Atiernan," another man's voice hissed from the chaos. "You have to scry her."

Ben nodded his agreement. "It is the only way. The only way to know just who she's working with, what she told them—if anything. You'd even be able to find the source of the sentinels."

More sounds of agreement. A few heads bowed in nods.

"I agree," chimed in a darkly cool voice.

Atiernan turned to find none other than Sanna, leaning against the open doorway with molten eyes.

Even the mortals knew the danger they faced—they had been betrayed. Someone had to be punished.

"It's the only way," Ben added venomously. "You must scry her. It may not be too late."

And damn it, Atiernan agreed. If the woman had dared to deceive him, betrayed him—then only death awaited her.

There would be no more second chances.

No more mercy.

No more…

"She saved me." The sound, so quiet it could have been the squeak of a mouse, had come from Beth. Shivering, the young daemon lifted her head to meet the accusing stares of her pack.

"She saved me…Miranda…she saved me."

At her words, everyone went silent. Atiernan bent low on one knee, leaning closer to hear her.

"Beth?"

"It was going to…to kill me," the girl went on calmly, almost in a daze. Atiernan doubted she even knew where she was. "She stopped it from…she *protected* me."

"The girl's delirious," Ben hissed scathingly.

"Or in shock," another man added with a shrug. "Either way, it doesn't matter—"

"Atiernan."

Beth's pale hand fell softly upon his cheek. "See," she said, willing her thoughts into his.

And he saw… He saw Beth run, drawn by a scream of pain, into the room where the creature lay in wait, crouched behind a terrified Miranda whose legs were covered in blood.

Already there was so much blood.

He saw Miranda shout at Beth to run. *Run!* He felt Beth's paralyzing fear. If she didn't move, she'd die. It was a cruel realization for someone her age to come to. Atiernan hated himself for not being there.

Through the fledgling's memories, he saw the creature howl as it caught her scent, cocking its deformed head to zone in on her with red eyes. A frantic thought had run through her head then—*I'm going to die.* And Atiernan had to agree with her. Immobilized as she was, the young daemon would have been easy prey.

Once again, Miranda shouted to *run*, screamed it. But, in the end, the witch was the first to move as the creature pounced, blocking its path with her own body, sacrificing herself in a spray of blood, and a scream of pain...

"Enough," Atiernan said quietly, extracting himself from the girl's thoughts. If they were to be believed, Miranda had been as caught off guard by the attack as they were. Though, she had been the first one to come upon the creature, coincidentally close to where it entered the manor in the first place.

"Atiernan?" Beth croaked, drawing his attention back to her.

"Get her up to bed," he told the woman comforting her. "Keep her safe—stay with her. But don't let Peony know. Not yet."

He doubted the mage would want to hear it from anyone else.

To his men, he sighed and turned his head to face them all.

"Your fears and accusations do not go unheard," he began in a voice like iron.

"And?" Benjamin pressed.

With another forced sigh, Atiernan pulled himself to his full height. "I will call a tribunal to deal with Miranda," he said finally, ignoring the gasps and mutters that erupted at his words.

It was the oldest set of laws his kind had—an ancient court called only when lives were threatened—when the safety of the entire pack was on the line.

He would call a tribunal, and the fate of Miranda would be out of his hands.

If she had truly done this, Atiernan didn't even want to think of the punishment that awaited her.

He wouldn't be able to help her now. She was at the mercy of his pack.

At the mercy of *their* justice.

Gods help her if she had dared to betray him.

EIGHTEEN

Miranda ran headlong through a wave of mist, feeling brambles and thorns snag at her hair and bite into her flesh. It was dark, and cold. She couldn't see more than a foot in front of her, and she was barefoot, tripping over roots and weeds—searching.

For what exactly?

She had no idea, but it was important—life or death. She knew that much. Desperation drove her on, but a part of her sensed she would never find this elusive thing. It was like smoke, escaping her at every turn.

Though, the pain in her body was making it hard to see *anything*. Suddenly, the nightmare broke, but—as she regained her senses—reality didn't seem any better. A horrible pressure assaulted her throat—a tearing, wrenching pain that itched like hellfire.

She raised a hand to scratch it, but a firm voice stopped her.

"You don't want to do that."

Miranda blinked her eyes open as someone grabbed her wrist and lowered it to her side.

"Trust me," the figure calmly insisted. "It took me four hours to seal those wounds. Luckily, your bones healed quickly enough, but sealing flesh is tricky. Were I a real witch, I might have more faith in my skills. As it stands, one wrong move might undo my hard work, and I won't risk it. Rest."

Her vision cleared enough to reveal the stern face of the mage, Peony, hovering over her like a pale apparition. Her long hair hung loosely, tickling the skin of Miranda's throbbing shoulder.

"It hurts," she croaked, flinching away. Every bone seemed to throb. She felt like she'd been dragged through hell and eaten by daemons along the way.

Peony didn't reply. Instead, the ageless woman turned to a nightstand laden with mysterious objects and withdrew a folded strip of cloth which she then soaked in a bowl of water.

"Here—" She dabbed the cloth along Miranda's burning forehead. "It's *helmps root*," Peony explained, gingerly wiping her chin next. "It may help the pain."

Miranda frowned. An herb that potent was only used to treat extreme injuries, typically as a last resort. Uneasy, she tried to sit up, only to fail as her limbs refused to obey the simplest of commands.

"My neck," she managed to croak. "What happened?"

Peony rewet her cloth and wrung out the reddish liquid. "You don't remember?"

Miranda could only shake her head. "No."

Her thoughts were a nonsensical blur. It hurt to try and decipher them. Somehow, she'd wound up here, lying on a bed in a room way too large and well-lit to be her cell.

"You were attacked," the daemon admitted. "Sentinel bites tend to be fatal to mortals. Luckily for me, you seemed to respond to our treatment methods rather well for a witch. Though, you must take care with your throat. The stitches will dissolve on their own, but I won't be willing to replace any should you tear them before you've healed."

What those methods were exactly? She didn't elaborate, and Miranda was too uneasy to ask. At the woman's words, it all came rushing back. Everything.

The sentinel, the blood, the burning pain…

But one fear stuck out in Miranda's mind the most.

"Is she alright?" Ignoring the pain that nearly split her in two, she pulled herself upright as far as she could. Another glance around the room revealed no one else in view, and her throat tightened with dread. "The girl? Is she alright?"

"Who?" Peony tried to push her back down, but Miranda shrugged her off.

"The girl," she rasped, recalling the memory clearly. "It was going for the girl…"

"What girl?" Peony's eyes widened. "*What* girl?"

"She's fine, Peony—"

Both women turned to the door, which was now open, revealing a figure who stood in the shadows. Even with his face obscured, he required no introduction. Slowly, he advanced over the threshold, so tall his head nearly brushed the ceiling as he closed the door behind him.

Atiernan.

"It's late." His eyes were grim as he turned to Peony. "I'll stay here. You go to Beth."

At the sound of her daughter's name, Peony withdrew from the bed with the washcloth still clenched in her hand. "Bethaem?"

Atiernan sighed, raking a hand through his hair. It was a rare show of unease, and Miranda felt her heart pound ominously at the sight.

"She's fine," he insisted finally. "But she needs you. I will stay here—Merye has taken her to your room."

Peony was halfway to the door before he'd even finished talking. As she passed the warrior, she pressed the sodden rag into his hand and nodded meaningfully in Miranda's direction. "I'll bring more bandages," she said, and then she was gone.

Childishly, Miranda wished she could follow her rather than be left alone with the warrior. At least the girl was alive. She couldn't bear to think that she had lived while someone so innocent had not.

Though, thinking of the pain in her throat, she couldn't imagine how she still was. Because of Peony? Confused, she eyed the ceiling, her body tense with anticipation.

Suddenly, cool fingers brushed the sweat-damp hair from her brow, and once again, she could feel the soothing effects of the *helmps root* working into her skin.

But this touch held none of the brisk efficiency of Peony's.

She didn't dare look over at the culprit, or even speak. All she could do was endure the stiff ministrations. Once he presumably set the rag aside, he brought the rim of a glass bottle to her mouth.

"Drink," he ordered.

Miranda obeyed, though it could have been poison for all she knew. The liquid burned slightly going down her throat, but the remaining pain instantly ebbed. Enough that she could roll onto her side and touch her neck as gently as she dared. A bristly surface met her fingertips instead of smooth flesh—stitches, she realized. *Many* stitches trailing down the length of her shoulder.

The scars would be gruesome, more than the ones on her arms were. Oddly enough, vanity was the furthest thing from her mind.

"I don't need your help." She swiped back a thick layer of blankets and rose from the bed on trembling legs. "I need to work. Where is the creature's body? I can inspect it for information on who crafted the spell responsible. Hurry, before it decays beyond all use. Show me." She barely managed one step before her knees buckled.

In the next instant, she found herself swept off her feet...

And lifted into thick arms that held her as though she weighed nothing. "You aren't going anywhere," her captor grumbled near her ear.

"Let me go." She swore at him, voice hoarse, but her attempts to fight him off were laughable.

In the end, her hand swiped weakly at his forearm, but she wound up marveling at the thick muscle twitching beneath her palm. If she didn't loathe the man, she would have requested his assistance. Someone like him would have no trouble dissecting any beast.

But she could fare on her own as long as she began in time.

"Do you want my help or not?" she demanded, craning her neck to meet his gaze despite a twinge of pain. "I don't need to be coddled. I need to work—"

"The beast should be the least of your problems," he snarled over her, dropping her unceremoniously onto the mattress. "We have evidence that the beast was allowed inside by someone via the kitchens."

"That makes sense," Miranda croaked—and the prospect brought with it a whole new level of danger. Had one of the daemons been so reckless? Or perhaps she herself had witnessed the one responsible? The memory was hazy, but with every passing second, she grew more convinced of what she saw—another man inside the manor.

"Does it?" Atiernan countered. He didn't appear to appreciate her easy acceptance of his theory. "Whoever is responsible for such a crime would have to be beyond reckless," he went on. "Perhaps they didn't understand the consequences of what they'd done until it was too late?"

Miranda disagreed. She saw up close how vicious that monster had been. If she hadn't been there when that poor girl came across it...

Who knew what would have happened?

"You daemons may be strange creatures, but I don't think anyone could let such a monster inside without realizing the danger it would put everyone in," she replied.

"Exactly," the daemon lord agreed, but his tone dropped an octave, suddenly cold. "To find the culprit, I've called a tribunal. If you are found guilty, I pray your gods help you."

"A what?" The term made Miranda's head pound. Then she processed the second half of his statement. "You think... You think I did it?"

Taking advantage of her confusion, Atiernan came to stand before her, leaving no escape from his cold stare. "Enough games, witch. Did you let the sentinel in?"

Miranda blinked. "What?"

His fangs flashed as he snarled each word with lethal clarity. "Did. You. Let. It. In?"

It, being the sentinel? She couldn't silence a harsh laugh that the daemon didn't return. "Are you insane?"

"Do not play stupid, Miranda. It does not suit you."

"Then yes," she snarled. "I let the monster in. Then I stuck around to sacrifice myself to save a daemon girl for the hell of it."

He winced, and she realized he already knew that part of the story. Apparently, gratitude wasn't enough to free her from guilt in his mind.

"I don't presume to understand the motives of you witches," he replied.

But that was only part of the reason. The truth was that he didn't think she was above threatening the life of a child just to harm him and his people. Though, she hadn't exactly spewed peace and love toward the race when she arrived, had she?

"How could you even think…"

"How *couldn't* I?" he bellowed. "You all but swore to destroy me, remember? Tonight, you almost did."

His words weren't entirely for show. He looked worn. His hair was disheveled, and his left pantleg sported a jagged gash. Far more concerning were the dark stains dotting his black shirt. Blood.

Hers?

Whatever the cause, it wasn't lost on her that for the daemon to let her see him in this state…he must have been at his wit's end.

"I didn't let the monster in," she croaked. "I swear it."

"If you did…"

He trailed off, letting the ominous silence speak for him.

"Wait," Miranda croaked. "I can prove it."

He scoffed. "I thought you witches were more creative with your lies—"

"I think I know who did," she said in a rush. Her recollections were a jumbled mess, but one image stood out, surprisingly clear—that of a man. "Let me see the creature's body. You might find a knife wound there. That can prove it!"

Atiernan watched her impassively, and she feared he might kill her regardless.

"The creature has been burned," he said. "But I don't understand why you think a knife wound would absolve you of guilt…"

As the seconds ticked by, she recognized that he was giving her time to speak.

"There was a man." The memories were still hazy, but she could pick out one detail to prove her innocence at least. "He wasn't a daemon. I don't think. He attacked the monster, but then he vanished. I don't know where he went—" As the words left her mouth, she realized how insane she sounded. The only alternative, though, was to accept the brand of a traitor. "He had dark hair. A knife. And—"

"You saw him in the house?" Atiernan responded. It wasn't an outright denial. Watching him, Miranda was willing to go so far as to suspect the man might have believed her.

"Yes." She nodded, her stomach tight. Was this relief? "I don't know where he went, but I swear on my life I didn't let the creature in."

"This man... You said he had dark hair. Describe him in detail."

She swallowed, wracking her brain. "He was tall. Fairly young, perhaps in his thirties. His features were..." She trailed off, noting the facial structure of the man before her. "He looked like you."

Atiernan turned away, and Miranda steeled herself for his reaction. Anger?

"Your cohort, perhaps?" he asked offhandedly. Before she could respond, he whirled to face her. "Let's assume I believe you. Can you track this intruder?"

She hesitated, weighing which answer would appeal to him most. The truth? "I don't know. Not without my magic, at least. And without the monster's body, it would be hard to track someone who—"

"You will," Atiernan replied. "Find this stranger and bring him to me, or I will find the answers myself if I have to."

She paled at the insinuation. He would scry her.

"I suggest you move quickly, witch." He started for the door only to pause with the same realization Miranda figured came to her mind.

His gaze went to her bracelet, and before she could react, he was at her side, gripping her wrist. With brute strength, he crushed the ornate metallic design at the center of the piece, shattering the entire thing.

"Use your magic on me, and you will regret it," he warned, releasing her. "But don't savor your freedom for long, witch. Find this intruder. Your very life depends on it."

She believed him without a doubt. And, as the remnants of the bracelet fell away, she couldn't even bring herself to feel triumphant at having her power returned.

There just wasn't time.

The second Atiernan's footsteps faded from earshot, she stood and inspected the room she found herself in. There was a bathroom attached, and someone, most likely Peony, had left some folded clothing on the counter along with a set of underwear. The plain gray dress with short sleeves wasn't exactly fashionable, but it wasn't meant for a child, at least.

She took her time washing the blood from her skin before peering into the mirror hanging above the sink. Peony hadn't been lying—while not a witch, her attempts to seal the wounds were impressive. Apart from a neat row of black stitches, none would know how extensive her injuries had truly been.

She felt a tendril of gratitude before pride suppressed it.

Peony, like Atiernan, just wanted something from her, be it her help or her knowledge. Well, thanks to the warrior, the tables had turned, and they were now on an even footing.

Not that she was foolish enough to call on her power now.

Instead, she dressed and returned to the bedroom, spotting a lone window that displayed a view of the outside world. It was a crisp morning, the perfect setting to prove her innocence to a smug daemon lord.

If the bastard wanted answers, there wasn't time to waste.

And it wouldn't do any good to wait for his permission to find them, either.

CHAPTER
NINETEEN

A sentinel inside the manor walls.

An intruder who happened to look like him.

Damn. As the various threats against him and his people mounted, Atiernan found himself grappling for a solution. Something needed to be done—even if it meant impulsively returning Miranda's power without weighing the consequences.

Luckily for her, the witch was no longer his sole concern. For the first time in years, he felt…uneasy. The impulses he'd spent millennia controlling were threatening to resurface with every passing second. Miranda's blood had been the mere tipping point. His fangs ached, constantly extended. He wanted to bite. Destroy. Rip. Tear.

Damn waiting patiently for answers, he wanted blood.

For now, he'd start with investigating the witch's story. Presumably, she saw a man that coincidentally looked like the figure he saw in the slain sentinel's memories. Could they be the same person?

He doubted it. The fortress was enchanted. No one short of an expert mage—or witch, in fact—could break those protective bonds unnoticed. Not even an average daemon could amass that kind of magic. Unless, of course, he had a witch consort. Atiernan couldn't take credit for the wards. No, they had been erected thousands of years ago on this plot of land by the very woman he once thought would be by his side for eternity.

Liva... Even thinking of her name inspired a wealth of reactions he couldn't compare to anyone else. Not even Miranda.

Though, they were from the same coven. Now, more than ever, that knowledge itched at him. After all this time, he had no idea if she were still alive—though, on second thought, he had no doubt she would be.

Liva was a force, unlike anyone he'd ever encountered. And if anyone would know how to engineer a hoard of vicious sentinels skilled in evading her own protection spell...

He growled at the possibility. After centuries of silence, Liva had chosen to target him. But why? And who had she used as her proxy? The appearance of the man unnerved him. As he neared his study, he spotted Benjamin and gestured him over.

"I want the manor searched from top to bottom. Every room. Every inch."

If there were an intruder, he would find them.

"Sir." Benjamin hesitated. "What about the witch?"

He frowned. Miranda was still a threat, even if he refused to acknowledge just how dangerous she could be. He'd avoided one glaring way Liva could have circumvented her own protection spell.

Via another witch, of course—one from the same damn coven. He told himself he'd chosen her at random, but that would be a lie. The second he decided to capture a witch, he'd gone into the mortal realm himself rather than delegate the task to someone else.

He alone watched her. For days he observed that coven, homing in on the strange, plain woman with dark hair who seemed both revered and mistrusted by those in her orbit.

Even now, he could picture her clearly—dressed in the modest clothing witches preferred, her hair unbound. She spent hours out in the fields, combing through various plants with the care most women tended to their children with.

He could lie to himself and deny it, but she'd enthralled him from the very moment he saw her.

She wasn't like Liva. She wasn't bold and breathtaking and able to command utter devotion with a wink and a grin. No... Even from afar, Miranda's effect on those around her had been apparent. They hated her as much as they respected her. Feared her, too.

That hostility drew him to her like a moth to a flame. He'd naïvely thought that a woman like that couldn't cause anywhere near the damage Liva had.

But Liva certainly knew him well enough to craft a convincing decoy. Another witch who he would unknowingly bring into the heart of his territory.

And then bestow upon said woman her full powers.

"Lord Atiernan?"

He stiffened as Benjamin returned before him, his expression worried.

"What is it?"

"The witch… She isn't in the room you left her in, sir. And we found this—" He lifted the remains of the binding bracelet.

Atiernan was too lost in thought to explain that he himself had removed it. *Damn.* Fear, unlike anything else, ripped through him, stealing every ounce of air from his lungs. For a heartbeat, he visualized the destruction Liva could unleash. Death. Bloodshed. All his fault because he let himself be outsmarted once again.

Just as the terror took hold, a darker emotion smothered every trace. No. He was not the same man he'd been when Liva nearly destroyed him. Miranda had been faced with his caricature of a daemon lord until now, but it was time for him to take off the mask and reveal the warrior lurking beneath.

The true Atiernan.

She and Liva may have plotted and schemed to deceive him so far, but no more.

He inhaled, dragging remnants of that teasing scent into his lungs. At her core, Miranda was just a witch, and he was a Raeth. He would find her.

And, once he did, he would rip her to pieces.

TWENTY

By sneaking outside of the manor, Miranda knew she was playing a dangerous game. Just a day prior, she wouldn't have dreamt of doing something so reckless. So insane.

To toy with the patience of a man like Atiernan…

There better be a damn good reason. Sadly, all she could come up with was one—desperation. Good gods, she needed to feel the wind on her skin and taste the fresh air. It was a craving no amount of fear could erase. Impulsive. Instinctive. Days without her power, and it was almost greedily that she drew upon it—though not to escape the manor itself as she should have.

She merely used a simple levitating spell to leave the looming fortress via the window. As the damp earth squelched beneath her bare feet, she couldn't regret the action. Besides, this was the only way she could help the daemon find the answers he sought.

Viewed from the outside, the towering structure was impressive. Made of dark gray stone, it rose from a hill like a castle, overlooking a dense swath of forest that stretched on for as far as the eye could see. Within its protection, she could easily picture decades of families living here, under Atiernan's control.

The man was ancient, after all. While daemons and their ilk weren't openly discussed among those in the coven, she still knew the stories. The legends, and the nightmares told to children to keep them in line.

Of the Blood Warrior. Atiernan the Terrible. Uninspired name aside, even hearing the stories as a young child, Miranda knew that such a simple word was all that was necessary to describe such a man. One who killed indiscriminately. Who sowed fear and destruction wherever he went.

Lucifer's righthand man.

Now that she'd met him for herself, a part of her wanted to scoff at those fearsome legends. He was nothing like those horrid depictions. If anything, she could admit that he seemed more civilized than most men she'd had the unfortunate pleasure of meeting.

And that was what scared her. His…humanness. The way he spoke to her without judgment, or even disgust. The fact that he allowed her some small semblance of freedom at all.

Few witches had ever spared her that same amount of grace.

And yet, she could sense something lurking within him—a monstrous force every bit as vicious as the legends claimed. For now, he kept such impulses at bay, but for how long?

She wasn't inclined to find out.

For that reason alone, she should have mustered her power to teleport from this accursed place no matter the risk. Logically, it would be a foolish endeavor to try—while she hadn't mentioned it to Atiernan directly, she knew she wasn't the only witch to visit these lands. A long time ago, one put a safeguard over this place.

It was old magic. Stuff the covens didn't teach anymore and was only practiced by rogue mages. She doubted she could easily circumvent it, not without time and study of the runes that bound the spell.

Luckily, the wards alone couldn't prevent her from her current task.

She inched forward, dipping beneath the dense tree cover. As if driven by instinct, she knew the second she reached the land where Atiernan and his men scattered the monster's ashes. The air reeked, and the earth looked grayed and decayed. Like death itself.

With a sigh, Miranda knelt and placed her fingers over the cool ground. Up above, a blue sky peeked between the swaying branches of the trees that obscured the rest of the landscape. Focusing on it, Miranda tapped into the stores of magic now free to her, but she only drew on a tendril. Enough to sense the fading life force of the sentinel that once was whole.

There wasn't much left. If the creature hadn't been burned, she might have gotten far more. Still, she could catch fragments.

The magic that drew the beast here was…

Primal. Sloppy. Not the neat, orderly spells she was used to composing. To put it bluntly—it wasn't like words written on a page, but runes carved into stone. Hard to decipher, and yet far stronger than paper.

They were formed by a witch. One who knew a darker strain of magic than any she was familiar with. Something ancient, sealed with…

She gasped and recoiled as the origin of the magic came to her. This wasn't formed with potions and herbs, or even a simple spell. This was something much more arcane.

A forbidden taboo.

The potential complications of such a spell confounded her. She barely even noticed the thud of heavy footsteps approaching until it was far too late.

"Should I kill you now?" The guttural voice road a gentle breeze that ruffled her tangled hair and soothed the skin around her wounds.

Alarmed, she lurched to her feet and spun to find a being of perfection stalking through the woods in her direction.

Within the manor, he was handsome. Out here, bathed shamelessly in the sunlight, this man was breathtaking.

Miranda felt her lips part as she took him in. Then his words registered, as well as the open hostility in his tone.

"I wasn't… I'm not leaving," she stammered. Drawing herself upright, she smoothed a hand along her borrowed dress. "I told you I needed access to the creature's remains. I wanted to see if I could find the source of the magic that sent it."

She expected anger. Mistrust. Not shock. It was a fleeting thing to witness—just a glimmer in his amber eyes. A heartbeat later, he'd already recovered, inclining his head.

"And did you?"

She hesitated. He certainly didn't trust her. And to even suggest something so strange. The implications could be momentous.

Though, when Atiernan's eyes narrowed, she offered up a halting reply, "I think this creature was controlled using blood magic. It's a forbidden art, far more powerful than any spell an average witch might know and very crude. They would need a tie to the target of the spell. Your blood would be a suitable anchor, for instance."

"You think I wouldn't know if someone drew my blood recently?"

Miranda choked, her cheeks flaming. He had a point. The way he'd so eagerly drunk from her made her head spin. She couldn't imagine anyone, not even another daemon, getting close enough to feed from him. Unless…

"A lover," she croaked. "They wouldn't need much, only a drop."

A sound rumbled from his throat, thick and grated. It was a second before she realized what it was—laughter.

"I have no lover," he said. "Not in millennia."

"You expect me to believe that?" She couldn't help the disgust in her voice. A man like him probably took paramours regularly—and that was putting it in the politest of terms. "I am not so sheltered that I blush at the knowledge of men and their pastimes," she added in a hiss.

She expected annoyance in return, at best. Not for him to raise an eyebrow and shoot her a glance that made her sway, suddenly breathless.

"You think I care to lie to a witch about who I fuck and when?"

"Of course not." She turned away, eyeing the scorched earth at her feet. "I only meant…"

"No one has taken my blood, a lover or otherwise. Trust that I would know," Atiernan said coldly. "If this is your way of convincing me to let you sample a drop yourself, you've failed."

She shuddered, horrified. "No, as if I would ever resort to such methods! If not your blood, then someone else is the source. Someone within the fortress is being used as an anchor to draw the sentinels here. Until that link is severed, they will continue to come."

"And you?" An unexpected warmth on her sore neck was her only warning as he spoke from behind her, alarmingly close. "Are you the 'anchor' drawing those creatures here?"

She had no chance to respond.

Within seconds, he had her pressed against the unyielding bark of a tree, facing him. He should have looked unholy bathed in sunlight. Not...

So damn beautiful, even with his fangs freely bared, gleaming ivory. A part of her knew instinctively what he planned to do. Her throat tensed, readying for a scream— but her body reacted all wrong. She tilted her head instead, exposing the flesh to him, even as a part of her reeled at the action.

His eyes lowered, scanning the offering. Rather than ravenous, he looked disgusted.

"You use your magic to escape my guards, but not to heal yourself?"

She flinched, alarmed by what could have been a genuine note of concern in his voice. Did he want her to?

Not that it mattered.

"Witches can't use transformative magic on ourselves," she explained hoarsely. "Only on one another. It's why we live in covens—" She broke off, horrified as her words died on the wind.

It was too late. He'd already gleaned more than enough to use the knowledge against her.

And his slow, ripe smile warned that he craved nothing more than to do just that. "So if I make you bleed… Make you hurt. You'll be forced to suffer?"

She shivered, unable to meet his gaze. "And you would enjoy that, I'm sure," she snarled, feeling her eyes burn with rage. "Hurting me, you brute—"

"Anything to expose such a foolish lie."

His hands. She recognized the shape of them on her hips, though she didn't dare look down to see them there for herself. The fabric of her dress was tissue-paper thin against him, his heat mesmerizing. Raeth daemons weren't known to radiate warmth. They were cold creatures, feeding on the living.

Atiernan, however, felt anything but lifeless. No, he felt dangerous. His fingers were so heavy, settling over the delicate bones that seemed liable to break at the slightest pressure.

In vain, she tried to wiggle from his grasp. "D-Don't touch me—"

"I've known witches before," he growled, cutting her off. "Witches who could keep themselves young, beautiful, and healthy with no difficulty."

Miranda frowned, shocked enough to meet his gaze. "Then you never knew a real witch," she hissed. "Nature's energy could never be used for such vain endeavors. That is blood magic—"

His expression silenced her mid-word. He wasn't angry or enraged. Instead, he looked as though she'd presented an answer to a confounding puzzle. His eyes widened, but his mouth formed a hard line that chilled her to the very core.

"Explain," he demanded.

Miranda bristled at the command, but something wouldn't let her retort nastily, the way she wanted to.

"Witches are servants of nature. Our magic is bound by the old laws, and therefore we can only heal, nurture, and do no harm. There are ways a witch can circumvent the limits of our practice, of course," she admitted. "But they are taboo. Old magic, accessed only with a blood sacrifice. If you knew a witch who did such things, she was no witch I would call a sister of mine."

A grudging tilt to his smirk betrayed that he believed her. Still, he laughed again. "Funny, considering that she came from the same coven you belong to."

Miranda blinked. "I know of no witch who has left our coven recently."

And the way he referred to this woman... It proved him a liar in more ways than one.

"But she was your lover," she suspected out loud. "And I'm sure she had the perfect chance to take your blood in multiple ways—"

His grip tightened on her waist. Not enough to hurt. Just enough to make her wince.

"The last time I saw that witch, your ancestor was but a distant thought in the mind of some peasant, centuries in the past. I'm sure, for use in blood magic, a sample must be fresh, no?"

He had a point, and her mind reeled at the reality of having a logical discussion about magical constraints with a daemon—especially one with the centuries of knowledge he seemed to possess. She could barely keep up with the conversation. "Not necessarily. Not if... If you had a blood-line from which to siphon a sample. That ancestor of mine you mentioned, if they were still alive, I could serve as a link to them, if someone knew the right spell."

And she was sure he had plenty of bloodlines sired throughout the ages. Rather than look smug, he grimaced.

"Then your explanation loses even more substance as I have no living bloodline."

He sounded convincing enough. But... Her mind conjured the image of the man she saw. Had she imagined him? No. Eyes like that couldn't be devised by her limited imagina-tion. He had been real, and his resemblance to the man before her was so uncanny she could only think of one explanation.

Somehow, they were related.

"Are you sure of that? A century alone is more than enough time to lose track of a wayward heir, let alone several," she pointed out.

She had enough tact to withhold the rumor that daemon men were known to be virile and careless with the resulting children. Her own father reinforced that belief.

Atiernan chuckled, but the sound was harsh. "Do I seem like a man who would abandon his own child?"

His voice was so heated her belly flipped. She had to shake her head to clear it. "The witch you mentioned. Who was she?"

As children, the girls in her coven were encouraged to memorize the name of every ancestor witch. It was a way to memorialize them, but mainly to learn from the mistakes of those who dared to stray from their path. She couldn't recall any who'd run off with a daemon, but there were a handful who'd gotten caught practicing blood magic, among other crimes.

Her bloodline, in particular, sported its own dark rumors where daemons were concerned. In fact, her namesake Miranda, had been a witch who lost her life to daemon magic and nearly destroyed the coven as a result.

"Why?" Atiernan countered. "So you can use your magic to summon her here and conspire against me?"

His use of present tense made her cock an eyebrow. "You think she's still alive?"

Though, she would have to be to create a spell capable of controlling the monsters—another hole in her theory. He was right to be skeptical—no witch could outlive millennia. To propose as much was his way of mocking her, surely.

This time, however, he wasn't laughing. "I'm *sure* she is, if she had the desire to. Even death would be no match for her."

Miranda swallowed. "Then I don't think the woman you knew was a witch."

"She was. Once." He released her and headed toward the fortress. Miranda was inclined to assume he no longer saw her as a threat, but that wasn't it. For the time being, he was fixated on someone he considered far more dangerous than she could ever be.

This mysterious woman from the coven of Hazel.

"Who?" she demanded, following after him. "No witch I've heard of has ever forsaken the craft completely. And to live this long? I don't know of a skill or magic one could utilize—"

"None that would appeal to your innocent sensibilities," he said with open scorn.

Curiosity kept her moving, even as her heart fluttered with every step taken. "A witch like that... I would know of her. Her name would be whispered with derision no matter the century. Especially if she came from my coven, as you claim. No witch from Hazel's Way would ever consort with a daemon. Live with one, anyway—"

"I was that daemon." His voice reached back to her, chilling and so finite she shuddered. "And I thoroughly knew that witch, in every way fit to make your cheeks blush, woman. I knew her. If she desired to live as long as I have, she would still be living. None of your gods, rules, or magic would stand in her way. I can assure you that."

"Fine." Miranda stumbled over a wayward branch, panting with the effort it took to match his long strides. "Then tell me her name."

He stood still, ablaze in golden light like a living, breathing flame. As much as it bothered her to admit, she couldn't imagine ever seeing anything or anyone more beautiful than he was.

"Liva," he said finally. "That was her name. Liva of Hazel's Way."

Miranda pursed her lips, unable to hide her disbelief. "I've never heard that name," she said. "Never. If she were from my coven, I would know her. We know all the names of the dead. All of the—"

He moved like a blur, already on her before she could blink.

"Your rules and your pathetic mortal ways! You don't understand what I am capable of—what *she* is capable of. You scoff at blood magic, but with one taste of the substance… We are unrestrained. Uncontrolled. You say Liva wasn't a part of your coven, but you are wrong. She founded that coven of Hazel, and I helped her find the very plot of land you all dwell on to this day. Even that precious tree your kind used to pray to. I helped her plant the damn thing myself, your namesake, in fact. A light wood—"

"Liar." Miranda scoffed. "If you prefer to play word games, daemon…"

But no. He looked haunted, and the weight of countless centuries was so apparent Miranda felt exhausted just looking at him. Her core foundation crumbled, and everything she thought she ever knew felt instantly called into question.

"Hazel's Way was founded by Mafalda Lightwood, *my* ancestor," she rasped. To her own ears, it sounded like a childish statement in the face of his claims.

"Lies," Atiernan snarled, his fangs bared.

The sight should have terrified her. To an extent, he always would—but after merely a few days in his orbit, she was beginning to sense when he was truly angry with her. And when his rage was directed elsewhere.

"No," Miranda argued, squaring her chin. "She was my ancestor—my family has carried that knowledge through generations, as many as I'm sure you've lived."

"I didn't bring you here to play semantics with mortal history," he replied. "Our concept of time varies vastly from yours, witch. I brought you here to find a solution. If you cannot find one, then I will *take* it from you, via any means necessary."

She wasn't a fool—it was a threat. One he'd merely hinted at before—and a danger she hadn't let herself truly contemplate until now.

"You mean you'll scry me." Her voice broke, and she hated him knowing just how much the prospect unnerved her.

Scrying was an ancient art, though some witches still practiced it—those banned from any recognized coven, of course. Blood magic was a more egregious taboo. Via either method, one could break into the mind of another living being and steal their memories, their thoughts.

And in doing so, the affected soul could be damaged forever.

"You're going to scry me," she croaked, pressing herself against a tree. Suddenly, her fragile hopes of understanding the daemon evaporated. He was a monster, just like the stories warned. "I'd rather you kill me instead."

"I will, should you give me reason to," he said. "You have one night to find the source of the attacks. I won't chain you or lock you away in the meantime. My guards will even give you free rein of the grounds. You can use your power how you see fit. Burn this manor to the ground and flee back to your coven if you want—but know this. I will find you. No matter how fast you run, I will find you. And I won't let pity restrain me then."

She shuddered as he turned away and headed for the fortress.

A part of her warned not to follow. Do what he claimed and run. Far far away.

A softer voice prevailed, one urging her to stay. To find the answer he wanted and to remain on his good side for as long as possible. She may have been a witch of Hazel's Way, but she knew in her soul that she was no match for Atiernan.

Not now. Not ever.

———)···•

Despite her wounds and growing exhaustion, she made it back inside her cell, fully expecting to find it empty. Instead, she nearly tripped over a small box someone had left on the floor beside her pallet.

Inside, she found a row of clean bandages and herbal ointment, most likely courtesy of Peony. Miranda didn't know if the unfamiliar sensation twisting in her belly was suspicion or...gratitude? The woman's gesture did serve as a reminder that this manor held plenty of ingredients useful in healing agents and potion making. A sudden impulse had her turn around and leave the dungeons entirely in search of a familiar room.

Atiernan had left her alone, but his men watched her, following at a distance as she reached a dusty storeroom on the first floor.

Peony wasn't inside, but Miranda was able to navigate her meticulously stored herbs and supplies alone. The monotonous work must have bored the guards, who eventually retreated from view, but she knew they weren't far.

Not that the observation stopped her at all.

Soon, she had a single potion bubbling away in the cauldron. It wasn't a potion of flight or one that would allow her to escape the fortress with her mind intact. No, this concoction was far simpler, but perhaps more vital in the long run.

She would play Atiernan's game and find his "solution."

And in the process, she would make the daemon indebted to her.

Indebted enough that she could make a bargain of her own.

TWENTY-ONE

He never slept at night. He merely waited for the worst of his exhaustion to pass—sometimes with his eyes closed and his mind in a lowered state of consciousness. Someone in his position, however, wasn't privy to the privilege of true slumber.

Unlike the mortal legends Miranda subscribed to, his kind were not so far removed from humanity as she seemed to think. They needed sustenance, and at least a few hours of rest per day. They could be injured, become ill and die should a wound prove grievous enough.

And, as much as it aggravated him to admit, his kind could *bleed*.

In the time he knew Liva, she would have had access to plenty of his blood. But enough to last thousands of years later? He doubted that. As for the other scenario the witch laid out…

No. If he had kin anywhere, he would know it. Liva wasn't that clever. Was she?

Damn the witch. For years he'd succeeded in driving that name from his skull entirely. Though, even she was no match against a new figure waiting to take her place. The owner of a scent that drove him wild.

Miranda Lightwood.

He groaned as traces of her aroma flooded his nostrils. His cock stiffened damn near instantly, his fangs protruding, aching to sink into that slender throat. The fact that he'd stopped himself at all was no small testament to his centuries-honed self-control.

But it was waning. His ultimatum to her had partly been out of self-preservation. One night—the longest he could keep from creeping into that dungeon where she slept and taking far more from her than answers to the sentinels' origins.

For a dangerous few seconds, he let himself toy with the idea of feeding from her, but his mind went further, revealing that craving for blood was only half of his attraction. He *really* wanted her breath on his neck. Her body writhing on his cock. Her soft lips on his...

He was a fool. She had to be utilizing her magic all this time, unfazed by the binding charm he'd saddled her with. With some twisted spell, she'd addled his brain and reduced him to a lustful idiot where she was concerned.

A part of him almost wished she had. That would give him a reason to retaliate. To teach the little witch just how foolish she'd been to play with fire. He'd corner her in that cell, wrap his hands around her throat and force her to beg. To say his name and plead for mercy. To murmur...

"So much for your grand claims," someone with a voice suspiciously like the witch's snarled nearby. "You're just like any other daemon. A liar."

He opened his eyes slowly, unconvinced that the real woman truly stood there at the foot of his bed, watching him with that haughty chin stuck in the air. Then he inhaled, and his mouth watered as her scent crawled into his lungs. He took in the pulse twitching in her throat and saw those dark little eyes dart to his bare chest.

Would the witch recognize the designs that composed his various tattoos?

At first, he wondered how she'd found his room among the many in the manor. Then he remembered... Peony had brought her here after the attack, though a maid had already erased all traces of her blood.

No bother. He had a supply of far more within reach. To her credit, Miranda seemed to realize the mistake she'd made by confronting him here alone. Too late. He lunged before she could move.

He barely remembered her original statement. All that mattered was the feel of her in his arms, so damn warm. He couldn't help himself—heedless of her cries, he pinned her beneath him and used a knee to part her legs as his lips nudged that sweet neck, taking care to approach from her uninjured side...

But she continued to speak, and finally, two words registered.

"...your bloodline!"

Surfacing from the bloodlust was harder than he could remember. Not since the days when he fed indiscriminately was it this damn painful to suppress the urge to hunt. He had to bite his own lip and grip the mattress beneath him to find the strength.

As his vision cleared, he was left facing the frightened witch, her chest heaving beneath him.

"You have a bloodline," she croaked. "That is the tether drawing the monsters to you. I confirmed it."

He pulled back, suddenly repulsed. Enticing scent or not, her personality alone repelled him unlike any other.

"You interrupt me to taunt me?" He couldn't keep the disgust from his voice. Damn her. Her pulse teased him even as he crossed the room, as beautiful as a song one could dance to.

"I interrupt you to call out your lie," she spat, still lying on her back. "You threaten me, but you withhold the truth. You sired a bloodline. I confirmed it."

He frowned. "It sounds like your magic deceived you, witch."

But no… Her eyes blazed, that haughty chin as pointed as ever.

"I did a spell to sense you and your kin specifically—"

He had his hand around her throat in an instant, silencing her without applying any pressure. He partially blamed Peony for the restraint—she would kill him should he ruin her handiwork. Pity played a role in why he held back as well. She was so damn delicate despite that sly, pink mouth. If he were inclined to seduce her, could her body even withstand the weight of his? He hated that his mind instantly conjured that image, and it wasn't exactly unappealing—her panting beneath him, those eyes so damn wide.

Then he realized just what she'd implied to him so openly.

"You used your magic on me?" He should have expected as much. Since when had fear alone stopped a curious witch from toying with his kind?

"N-No!" She paled at his tone, shaking her head. "Not on you exactly. You… You bit me. I used that mark to trace the source. You. Through that, I could divine any other living creature with the same bloodline."

"And you found something?" He didn't believe it. She had to be lying, spinning her web of deceit. At least he knew better than to ever feed from her again—and leave her alive afterward.

"Yes," she said breathlessly. "It's faint, but I'm confident. One other figure exists who shares your blood."

Lies. But her eyes… They gleamed with a light Atiernan had witnessed in a few others. Liva among them. The hallmark of a woman too damn clever for her own good.

She was telling him the truth.

"I can help you track them down," she went on as if reading his mind. "They might be the source of the sentinels."

"And in return, you want what?" He released her and stood back, crossing his arms. "Your freedom?"

She nodded, seizing her bottom lip between her teeth. His fangs ached just watching her. He could barely keep up with what she said next.

"That, and one more thing."

"Let me guess." He scoffed. "You want me as your attack dog? Your hired sword? So predictable are you witches, and yet so hesitant to face your numerous enemies alone."

Liva had been the same. And he had eagerly done her bidding every step of the way.

"No," Miranda insisted. "I want you to find something for me. You mentioned it yourself. The light wood tree."

"A tree." He raised an eyebrow. "What are you talking about?"

"Exactly that." She sat upright, smoothing a hand along her rumpled skirt. "The light wood tree. The one that grew on the spot upon which Hazel's Way was founded centuries ago. You claimed you were there. That you planted it—"

"What does a witch want with a tree? Doesn't your kind cloak yourselves in forests of them?"

She swallowed, darting her gaze to the floor at his feet. "Not the light wood trees. Not for many years. The last one was destroyed twenty-eight years ago. None have been found since."

It was such a trivial request he didn't know how to characterize it. A trick? It wasn't like he'd have to go out of his way to retrieve such a thing. Offhandedly, he admitted as much. "Peony probably has a clipping or a sapling—"

He didn't miss how her eyes widened. Much like his fantasy, only instead of his cock, just the mere mention of this tree brought her such pleasure. He loathed the sight of it. And yet...

"Why this?"

Her lips twitched, and he could see her weighing the risk of lying to him. He almost wanted her to, but when she opened her mouth again, he suspected that every word resonated with the truth.

"Because that tree is sacred to us in a way you can't imagine. If we could replant one in our grove... You have no idea what that would mean to my coven."

Her eager tone almost had him fooled. Almost.

"Not that," he said. "*You.* Why does this matter so much to you?"

Suddenly, she wasn't so haughty. Her eyes cut away from him, rousing a curiosity he couldn't deny.

"Tell me."

"I am a witch. A Hazel witch," she said softly. "My sole duty is to bring honor to my coven."

He grunted in alarm. She had no idea that years ago, another woman had said the same exact words to him. Words that turned out to be a lie. With such a tree, Liva had found a source of magic that allowed her to cease her reliance on his daemon blood. Miranda's aims were most likely the same.

He inhaled, prepared to deny her. No way in hell would he become the patsy of yet another conniving wench. As if anticipating that outcome, she stiffened, always on the defensive. He could even see her lips readying to form a sneer.

"Why can't you find this tree with your magic if you claim to have found a bloodline of mine?" he asked instead.

Caught off guard, she furrowed her brows. "That is what makes the tree so sacred," she said. "It is resistant to magic, able to form the strongest protection spells. No one in decades has been able to find a viable specimen. We've tried."

Inwardly, he mused at how she'd just innocently named the source of the spells protecting this very fortress. He could give Liva some credit in that aspect—her love had been a façade, but her magic wasn't.

"And armed with this tree, your little coven will regain its powerful status, won't it?" He laughed as a flush crept over her cheeks. "You think I'm not privy to your petty little politics? No, Miranda Lightwood. I didn't choose you at random. I watched your coven, and I surmised that, as much as they preach love and protection of all witches... They wouldn't come for you. So far, that calculation has proven correct."

As the words left his mouth, they merely served to cement the uncanny parallels between her and Liva. Both outcasts. Both too powerful for their own good.

And both he found irresistible for reasons he couldn't name.

Still, he took some small pleasure in watching how she reacted to having that truth flung in her face. She winced, and her eyes darted in that haunted way that warned she was terrified of what else he knew.

Admittedly, not much. Choosing her had been a conscious choice, but from the second he brought her to his dungeon, she'd thwarted every assumption he'd made. He had assumed a witch so isolated and ostracized from those in her coven would easily break.

She hadn't.

He'd thought her magic would be remedial at best, easily co-opted by Peony, who could manipulate her into fulfilling their true aim.

It wasn't.

And, more selfishly, he'd thought her plain features would cease to have any appeal to him—the polar opposite of Liva's breathtaking beauty.

Oh, how wrong he'd been.

"You've done your research," she retorted hoarsely. "I thought you daemons were dumb brutes who preferred violence over cunning. I was wrong."

He hadn't expected that. Yet again, she evaded his expectations.

"But, my usefulness to you hinges on my assistance, doesn't it?" she added, cocking her head. "The spell driving those monsters is strong—one of the most complex I have ever seen. You can kill me and steal another witch, but she wouldn't have a chance in hell of helping you. Not with all the magic in the world."

Her boldness amused him. "Oh? And what makes you better suited?"

Her eyes flashed. "I'm sure you know damn well why. That's the real reason you chose me, isn't it? Admit it now and drop the façade! You know exactly what I am."

Damn her. The reasons he gave were the sole ones he'd had in mind before capturing her. What else didn't he know? If he cared to think on it, perhaps why she'd been so ostracized in the first place. He knew vaguely that it had something to do with her parentage. Her father was unknown, and her mother, though influential in that coven, had extended very little of her protection toward Miranda.

Now, he wished he'd dug more into the reasons behind that gap. No matter. He could be persuasive when the urge struck him—and, around this woman, plenty of urges seemed to be emerging.

"Enlighten me, witch," he commanded, painfully aware of how his fangs teased his lower lip. "What are you?"

She swallowed at the sight, but still brandished that pointed chin. He could see the gears in her brain turning. Whatever she thought he knew, she was alarmed to realize that he didn't.

"I am a witch who knows blood magic," she said quickly. "I can assure you that no other witch who calls herself part of a coven can say the same."

As long-lived as he was, few things could ever catch him off guard. Yet, she had once again.

"And how would a little witch of Hazel know such magic?"

One explanation came to mind—she learned from Liva herself. Either way, her knowledge of the arcane was an outright confession of malicious intent—though, she didn't seem smug at her deception. Rather than form some haughty expression, her usually sly lips quivered.

"Because I do," she rasped. "You yourself said it—I was ostracized from the others. Because of that, I could learn things they wouldn't dare."

"A plausible enough story. Nonetheless, what's to stop me from binding your powers and throwing you into the dungeon to rot?"

Which he should have done, regardless of her reasoning. He even took a step toward her, but she flinched and clutched her hand to her chest—the one that had worn the binding charm.

"Please—"

For whatever reason, the breathless plea stopped him short.

"Don't… I can't go back there."

"Why not?"

"I'm afraid."

Her honesty confounded him. She was too much of a puzzle, worth more trouble than he'd bargained for. And yet…

He grasped a lock of her dark hair and twisted the strands between his fingers. "You think I should let you wander my manor unbound?"

"No," she admitted, surprising him. She even let the contact linger, though he knew it took every ounce of pride she still had left. "I'm asking for…"

She seemed unable to put exactly what she wanted into words. But he could guess.

"What are you willing to trade for access to your magic?" The demand was out of his mouth before he could question it. Greedily, his eyes traced that thin body, lingering over the delicate curves and narrow hips.

She stiffened, and he knew a nasty retort was coming.

"I...If you promise to find me the light wood tree, I will give... Anything."

He waited, expecting a laugh. A scoff. Any reaction at all to temper the animalistic part of him that growled in response to those words. A witch promising him anything.

There had to be a catch.

"Anything regarding myself," Miranda went on. "Not the coven, or using my magic for your aims—"

"Even sex?" he said harshly. "You should be careful, witch. Many daemons wouldn't give you the chance to clarify such a statement. You offer anything—they would take everything."

Her face reddened further, but to her credit, that chin never lowered even a fraction.

"My offer stands. In exchange for keeping my magic, and you helping me retrieve a viable light wood tree, I would give whatever you wanted."

His entire body went to war at the prospect. His fangs throbbed as his cock swelled at the thought. *Anything.*

Then he remembered that witches were deceitful creatures skilled at using their sexuality to their advantage.

"Go to your cell and wait for me," he commanded. In his own way, he was saving her from making a foolish bargain.

But she didn't run like she should have.

"Please," she pleaded, her tone unusually earnest. "Damn the consequences. I know what I'm saying. For that tree, I'd make a deal, with you or the devil himself!"

"Why?" He whirled on her and relished the tiny shiver she couldn't suppress. "Why is it so damn important to you? A few protection spells can't be worth your body. Your soul."

Whatever her reasons, he could tell from the set of her jaw that she wouldn't reveal them to him.

"Oh, don't play coy now, witch," he snarled. "You want to strike a bargain? You tell me everything."

He craved a fittingly devious answer. A handful came to mind easily—she wanted to use that tree to craft enough daemon-slaying weapons to kill hordes of his kind. She wanted power. World domination.

She was just like Liva.

"Our last tree was destroyed," she said softly. "Several of my kind have already lost their lives scouring the ends of the earth for a replacement. I couldn't call myself a witch of Hazel if I didn't do whatever I could to retrieve such a valuable piece of our heritage. That is all."

If witches were truly the paragons of virtue and nature they portrayed themselves to be, he might have believed that.

The reality was he knew better.

"No. There is more to it," he suspected. "Should I make that part of my answer to your bargain?"

And he would. Though, that would entail making a deal with the witch in the first place.

"Go to your cell," he said, though the order was no longer an escape route with her pride in mind. She'd gotten her wish. "If you want to prove yourself a willing partner, you will do so. Wait for me there. I'll even have food sent to you. Then, I will tell you if I've decided to accept your terms, and my price."

After a heartbeat, he heard her retreat without a word.

And he tried not to let greed override his common sense.

If Miranda wanted to play this game, then so be it.

He would name a price no witch would ever pay.

CHAPTER
TWENTY-TWO

She was a fool. A traitorous, selfish whore. There were other, more vicious words to describe her, but those would do for now.

What the hell had she been thinking?

Not like a witch, for damn sure. The daemons had done something to her. A poison slipped into her food to addle her brain? Or perhaps Atiernan himself had manipulated her thoughts when he fed from her?

It was a plausible explanation that spared her any guilt. *Yes, that was why she'd allowed him to take her blood in the first place*—he'd manipulated her thoughts. Bewitched her. And that alone was why his touch had felt so...good.

She shivered at the thought and brushed her fingers along her throat, skirting the fresh stitches. The flesh there tingled, but that wasn't the only part of her that came alive at the memory of the daemon's touch. The cleft between her legs ached in a way that made her press her knees together, desperate to ignore it.

Damn him.

For now, she explored the remnants of the fang marks, ignoring everything else. In comparison to the wound left behind by the sentinel, the punctures from Atiernan's fangs were minuscule.

And she had just signed up for more torture. More biting. More fear.

Before she learned of the possibility of a new light wood tree, she would have killed herself rather than submit to further abuse. No price was worth the dignity and soul of a witch.

But therein lay the irony—according to the rumors, she had no soul to begin with. She didn't doubt that Atiernan had done his research, but even he didn't seem to know the real reason for her exclusion from social life in the coven.

Thank the gods.

The truth went beyond any faux pas she might have committed. She'd been damned since birth, accursed for her own conception and upbringing. She'd always resigned herself to living on the outskirts of Hazel's Way despite her inherent strength and adeptness with magic.

But now…

It was childish to pin her hopes on something so far-fetched, but she couldn't help it. Bringing back a viable light wood tree to the coven's ancestral lands would be a boon no one could overlook. Not the elders. Not her mother.

No one.

They would have no choice but to accept such a token of her loyalty. Perhaps, they would even let her officially join their magical circles. For the first time in twenty-eight years of life, she saw the slimmest hope of a future without dodging scorn and derision. If the price was selling her soul to a literal daemon, then so be it. How had her existence before now been any better?

At least Atiernan seemed to relish taking her blood. He didn't curse at the sight of her. Even now, he didn't lock her in this cell and leave her to die should she refuse his commands. He didn't berate her.

Ungrateful beast! Thank the gods I let you live...

She shook her head to banish the memories before they could unfurl. No longer was she that helpless child, and any resentment she may have harbored had been long since buried. Regardless, she certainly took pleasure in imagining the crone's face should she be the one to restore the sacred tree.

For that privilege, she'd do anything. If the daemon wanted her body, so be it...

Though, she shied away from picturing the aftermath and focused on enduring the dark. Thankfully, the door to her cell was open, allowing the firelight from the main chamber to pierce the pitch-black darkness. It was enough to keep the panic at bay. Enough to help her think.

Until a shadow fell over the doorway.

"I've thought on your offer, witch." Atiernan's voice came from the darkness. "I won't take advantage of your naivety. You want your tree? I want you to find the source of the magic drawing the sentinels to my people and quickly. Nothing more."

Miranda didn't know what to think. Would it really be that easy?

No, claimed a lethal bit of laughter that trickled toward her next.

"And, I *will* take you up on your offer, at least partly," Atiernan declared. "You want your tree? Then for every minute it takes you to find the bastard behind this blood magic, I have access to your blood. As much as I want, via whichever method I so choose."

She cleared her throat, aware of the tender flesh. Whatever potion Peony had given her to dull the pain had yet to wear off, at least. She could endure another monster feeding from her if she had to.

"And that's it?" she asked.

Heavy footsteps made her jump as they advanced in her direction. In seconds, what little light there was vanished.

"You sound disappointed. Don't tell me you'd coddled yourself with fancies of rape and torture."

"Don't tell me you consider yourself above such base impulses," she snapped, but her voice was softer than she would have thought. Was that relief?

"No." He finally came into view, no less intimidating than the first day he met her here. "But I would be a fool to accept any offer of sex from a witch. I prefer to take from your body than give."

Her cheeks flamed at the insinuation. Rather than take the bait, she cleared her throat. "And the tree?"

"I'll relinquish it once you have fulfilled your end of the bargain."

He made it sound so simple, as if he had no idea as to the value of such a gift.

She blinked, unwilling to trust her own ears. "You mean you've found one?"

"No. I *have* one."

Her eyes widened, and for a second, she forgot the nature of her relationship with the daemon. She advanced toward him, seeking out his gaze. "What? Where?"

Somewhere in this fortress, most likely. Perhaps among the many trees she'd admired outside?

"Somewhere, you will not find it without my permission, witch," he replied.

Fair enough. As long as he gave her the tree, it didn't matter where it was stored.

"So when does it start?"

"Now."

He moved slowly, giving her ample time to run. He wanted her to. He wanted her to cry and scream and fall into hysterics—and a part of her longed to do just that.

It took every ounce of strength she had to remain standing and hold his gaze through the darkness. His eyes glowed like embers, feeding off what little light reached this corner. He was so massive she had to crane her neck back as he towered above, and his hands met the stone on either side of her head.

"Present your veins."

She flinched as her heart pounded against her chest. She couldn't breathe. His nearness was overwhelming, his voice alone terrifying, penetrating her deepest thoughts.

Still, she managed to arch her neck, allowing him access to the uninjured half. At the back of her mind, a million voices wailed in despair that she was a traitor. A whore. A bitch. Everything her mother claimed she would become and more.

Yet, one thought was enough to silence them. She alone would be able to do what none of the women who scorned her had. She would revive the sacred tree and right the wrong her birth wrought on the coven. Nothing could over-shadow that, not even submitting to the will of a daemon.

He grunted at her obedience, and she suspected he was disappointed by how easy she was making this for him. As his breath fanned her neck, she closed her eyes and waited for him to strike.

"Not there," he murmured.

She frowned, confused. Where else could he mean to feed?

"I'm sure you witches are educated in mortal anatomy," he taunted. "Tell me where the femoral vein is."

Her breath caught. He was correct. She knew anatomy. Enough to know that particular blood vessel was far below the throat.

Her lips parted, a refusal on her tongue. Somehow, she managed to swallow it down. Instead, she reached for the hem of her dress.

And he watched. She heard a low sound rumble in his chest as she fingered the fabric.

"Present it to me," he goaded, revealing that he was very much serious.

She bunched the skirt and raised it, exposing her thigh and the thin underwear she wore beneath. It was freezing in this room. Her body reacted, her nipples tightening.

But psychological torture seemed to interest him far more than feeding did. As the seconds ticked by, he never moved.

"I want you to say it," he prompted, as if reading her mind. "'Feed at your leisure, my lord.'"

She blanched at the phrasing. Was that what the so-called willing humans he kept here were coached to say? No. She suspected that even he wasn't that much of a narcissist. He wanted to hear those words from her alone.

Think of the coven, she thought in a mantra. *Think of the light wood tree. Think of Hazel's Way.*

And think of her mother, who would have no choice but to accept her should she return with such a sacred offering.

"Please, my lord," she croaked, meeting Atiernan's endless gaze. "Feed at your leisure—"

Before the words finished leaving her mouth, he crouched, gripping her waist in both hands. Her heart lurched at how big they felt. Powerful. Unnaturally hot, his breath teased her inner thigh. Then his teeth…

She gasped, squeezing her eyes shut in anticipation of the pain. Hell, a part of her *wanted* it to hurt. Unfortunately, this time was no different from the first. Instead of agony, she felt a tingling, electric sensation jolt up her spine. A shudder followed, making her knees buckle and sending those probing canines deeper. Every nerve prickled with awareness of his wet mouth…

Then he drank, so deeply her mind reeled.

And she forgot this was meant to be debasing.

She wished her body reacted with revulsion. Instead, her hips arched into him, and he grunted in approval, gripping her tighter. Individual fingers bit at her hips through the fabric of her dress, rivaling the feel of his lips feathering against her thigh. With slow, rhythmic movements, his tongue encouraged fresh blood to drip freely, but the resulting sensation was too much. Too sharp.

She whimpered as heat coiled in her abdomen, building between her legs with a vengeance. A writhing, hot pressure…

"Damn you, witch."

Her heart panged. Had she disappointed him? But no. As she looked down through fluttering eyelids, she found him crouched, still licking at droplets of her blood eagerly. More. More.

The desperation he fed with made her head spin. No man could be this ravenous. Not unless…

"So damn sweet," he groaned in between savoring laps of his tongue. "And so wet. I can smell you…"

His voice was deeper than she'd ever heard, even if his words made no sense. At least on the surface. Then she shifted her hips and felt the fabric of her panties cling to her sensitive flesh. Her cheeks flamed, even as her mind struggled to remember why she should be ashamed.

He had touched her there before—a searching pressure that made her throat go dry whenever she dared to recall it. Would he do so again, and take more than just her blood?

As if aware of her thoughts, he went still. She could hear every ragged inhalation of air he drew in. Hissed out.

It was as if he were tasting her essence in the air. With every drop of her scent, more of her body's traitorous yearning became clear to him. His fingers relaxed against her waist, no longer restraining. His mouth withdrew, and those scorching eyes lifted to meet hers.

"Ask for it, witch," he grated, his voice guttural. "Ask me for pleasure, and I will gladly give it to you."

Pleasure. The way his tongue caressed that one word made her head fall back against the wall, leaving her staring blindly through the darkness. He made it sound like a delicious promise—more powerful than any spell or potion she could ever compose.

And she wanted…

"Take my blood," she managed to croak. "Take what you wish… Just honor our bargain, daemon."

Abruptly, he pulled back and stood. Without a second glance, he stormed from the cell, leaving the door open.

Miranda didn't know whether to stay or follow. It was all she could do to remain upright as her knees buckled beneath her weight.

"You return to Peony within the hour, witch," the daemon commanded as his footsteps echoed throughout the dungeon. "Not a minute later."

Miranda leaned against the wall as the sounds of his retreat finally faded. Warmth dripped down her right leg at an alarming rate, but she couldn't bring herself to eye the wound.

It should have felt demeaning and degrading to be used as such.

Instead, she just felt dizzy.

CHAPTER

TWENTY-THREE

"It's you!" Peony looked up from her cauldron in genuine surprise as Miranda appeared at the mouth of her makeshift study. "Atiernan must have decided to let you roam free, after all."

Her raised eyebrow made it clear that the daemon lord hadn't enlightened her on their bargain yet. Miranda, however, was in no hurry to do so.

Instead, she squared her chin and tried to hold the mage's gaze without blushing. Her thigh ached still. She knew the daemon could smell the drying blood and chose not to comment on it.

Which somehow made it worse.

"I am to find the source of the blood magic drawing the sentinels here," she stammered. "To do so, I require certain herbs. Can you help me?"

It felt strange to ask for such help—especially when such a request would have been met with scorn back home.

"I can try." Peony shrugged and pushed her glasses further up the bridge of her nose. "My stores are limited compared to what you are used to, but I do have a decent array of items."

Like the sapling of a light wood tree, apparently. Rather than ask for it outright, Miranda focused on the task at hand.

"Show me?"

Peony beckoned her inside. In addition to the shelves out in the open, the woman had a chest kept in a back corner. After fishing a key from her tunic, she opened it to reveal a careful arrangement of materials that even Miranda was impressed with.

"You have a vast selection of supplies," she admitted.

Peony chuckled. "I may be a daemon, but if there is one advantage we have over you witches, it is an ability to amass ingredients not easily come by. What exactly do you need to trace this spell?"

Miranda hesitated. She wasn't a fool. Atiernan and his ilk would have every right to glean from her what they could and defend themselves *without* her help. Still, she took one small consolation in the fact that, for all her skill, Peony most definitely wasn't advanced in blood magic. That was a craft few could master, even those with the right intent.

You needed a vessel, after all, to supply the magic necessary. A creature with tainted blood.

"If I know what you have in mind, I can get a better idea of what you might need."

Peony's casual tone was enough to convince her.

"I plan to trace the origin of the spell. It will be difficult. I will need *nyrn* root and cipher's fern—"

"Can I suggest something?" Peony inclined her head, her expression thoughtful. "I'm assuming that you believe the source of the magic is something in this manor. Someone."

Miranda stiffened. Was Atiernan not the only one suspecting her of betrayal?

"I believe so."

"Then tell me, if not Atiernan, who?"

Miranda frowned. "He claims he has no bloodline. Perhaps he had a sibling long ago who sired descendants—"

"Or a child of his own?" Peony suggested, her mouth wrinkled in concentration. "A son."

Miranda nodded. "But he swears he never had any children."

"He wouldn't know." Suddenly, Peony stood with her face averted, her shoulders unusually tense. "But if he did… Could you trace them with your magic?"

"Yes," Miranda croaked. "But… What aren't you telling me?"

"I would hesitate if I thought for a second Atiernan would believe you," the woman admitted. "I know he would gut you on the spot should you even suggest the possibility. First, I ask you to hear me out. Then I will tell you what you need to form your spell."

Miranda didn't know how to process the offer. So much for her being Atiernan's blood supply until she found a solution to the sentinel attacks. Their bargain may be null and void already.

And she could return to Hazel's Way with one accomplishment no one could deny.

"I'll listen."

Peony led her to a distant part of her studio and gestured for her to take a wooden chair placed before a small table. The woman rummaged in another part of the room before sitting across from her, armed with two steaming mugs of tea.

"Drink," she instructed, placing one mug before Miranda. She turned to another part of the storeroom and called back, "I have some soup here too, if you'd like."

Seconds later, she placed a bowl of steaming food before Miranda as well. Thoughts of poisoning flitted across her mind, but she had to admit that between Atiernan and Peony, she trusted the woman more.

Warily, she sampled the tea, surprised by the pleasant taste. A heartbeat later, she drained the entire bowl of soup.

"Again, I warn you to never mention this to Atiernan," Peony said before sipping from her own drink. "Do you understand?"

Miranda nodded. "You said it yourself. He wouldn't believe me anyway."

"Even so, I would like you to swear it."

It wasn't like she had much left to lose. "I swear," she said, setting her mug down. "I will not repeat anything that you tell me."

Satisfied, Peony sighed and adjusted her glasses. "Atiernan had a lover once," she said. "Many years ago. Long enough that I hope the ravishes of time have erased her memory from this world. Her name was Liva."

Miranda sputtered, spraying tea all over the table. Given how gravely the mage seemed to relay this information, it alarmed her that Atiernan had told her so willingly. "I've heard."

Peony raised an eyebrow. "He told you?"

"He claimed that Liva founded my coven, but I've never heard that name—"

"You wouldn't have," Peony said with a dry laugh. "You witches are far pettier and more vindictive than my kind could ever be. I'm sure they've banished all trace of her name from your history books, but it is true. In fact, Liva founded many of the institutions your kind hold dear. And many of the threats you now fear. She was more dangerous than you can imagine, and I pray she's long dead. Though, even I am not so foolish as to believe that..."

She trailed off, staring wistfully into space.

Her obvious concern tempted Miranda enough to at least take her words seriously—though, on its face, the whole theory sounded insane. A mortal witch living millennia? "If she were alive, that would require magic I've never even heard of."

Peony nodded. "Which is why I wouldn't be surprised if she were. Back then, though, she was merely a frightened innocent witch that Atiernan rescued from the whims of her previous coven. They wanted to sacrifice her, you see, convinced that she was cursed by evil."

"Thank the gods we've outgrown such archaic practices," Miranda said dryly.

Nowadays, instead of sacrificing unwanted witches on a burning pyre, the elders shunned them from all aspects of daily life and tagged them with the term *"Saiga."* Which meant corrupted in the ancient tongue.

Would it have been easier in the long run if they killed her outright? Sometimes, she toyed with the idea that it might have been.

"Liva wasn't quite the victim she made herself seem," Peony said, drawing her attention back to the present. "Perhaps she deserved far more than a gruesome death. Luckily for her, a warrior from a neighboring tribe took pity upon her and rescued the witch, though their races were at war."

"Atiernan," Miranda suspected. She tried to envision the man risking his neck to help a witch. She could only come up with one explanation. "I'm sure she was beautiful, this Liva."

Peony nodded. "Beyond compare. The most beautiful woman you know wouldn't come close. It was her greatest weapon, you see. Few could accept that such a creature could be capable of such horror."

Miranda felt a twinge of jealousy. How privileged it must be to use your beauty as a shield against suspicion. Perhaps, if she had been born with enviable features, the witches might have given her a sliver of doubt? Cursed as she was with dark hair and darker eyes, they seemed to believe her features merely cemented the evil within her.

"Atiernan loved her?"

"Oh yes." Peony looked pained by the confession. "More than I think he will ever admit. She made him stronger than he could have hoped to be. She gave him the power to protect his people, and land he could call his own millennia later. But in return, she cursed him to an endless life and nearly destroyed his soul. But that is not my story to tell."

Miranda wasn't sure if she were genuinely curious. Perhaps her interest in Atiernan extended only to survival. As a child, she learned that her life was based on how quickly she could utilize the knowledge at her disposal.

Which was why she had a feeling exactly where Peony was truly headed.

"Are you implying that Atiernan had a child with this woman?"

"Drink," the daemon said, nodding toward her cooling tea.

Obediently, Miranda took another sip. Only then did Peony sigh and continue her tale.

"I never knew for sure, but a woman can sense things. But, by then, she was gone, and Atiernan required my sole focus. He was in no state to be bothered with trivial suspicions."

"If there was a child, do you really think their bloodline could last this long?"

Peony glanced at her sharply. "Daemons are not immortal, Miranda. There is a reason why Atiernan and I have persisted as long as we have, and it is not a blessing but a curse. Every day of this life, we are being punished for our sins, and I pray my daughter grows old and gray and dies after having lived her fair share of years. Not this soulless existence. If there were a child of Atiernan's, I hope it is long since gone."

"But you don't believe that," Miranda suspected.

Peony stroked her chin, her expression grim. "If there were a child and I told Atiernan, he would have gone to the ends of the earth to find the truth. Even if it killed him. Even if the cost was what little of his soul remained, he would have done anything. I thought that by withholding any suspicion, I was saving him. In reality, I could have allowed Liva a weapon he could never withstand. So, if there is a bloodline, I must ask of you one thing. You do not tell Atiernan."

"I already told him that he must have a living bloodline," Miranda admitted.

"Yes, but that isn't quite the same as confirming a direct lineage. Can you keep that from him?"

Miranda took her time responding. Allying against someone like Atiernan was a position she didn't consider lightly. "You want me to lie?"

"I want your silence."

"And what will you offer in return?"

"I can offer you protection," Peony said. "In more ways than one. I will not tell Atiernan the truth about you, for instance."

"W-What?" Miranda couldn't hide her alarm.

She hoped it was just a clever play on words—if Atiernan hadn't guessed her true nature, could Peony?

"I will admit I was fooled at first," Peony went on, a wry smile shaping her lips. "As he seems to be. But your scars give you away to those who know what to look for—" she nodded to the wrists Miranda desperately tried to cover beneath the infernally short sleeve of her dress. It was no use. "That and the fact that your body responded well to daemonic healing methods, which is the only reason you survived the sentinel's assault. Either way, I know what you are, girl. I can't imagine how hard your life must have been among that coven. Nor the pain you've experienced to garner those wounds—"

"Don't," Miranda hissed. Scorn and revulsion had plagued her entire life, but even she could admit that something else colored the mage's voice. Something far worse—pity. "Will you tell him?" she demanded, scouring Peony's dark eyes.

"No," the woman said. "Even if you betray our bargain, I will not tell him. He thought he'd taken a full-blooded pristine witch. If he realized his mistake, he might discard you in favor of another, and I can't have that. I think we have much to learn from each other yet. But I must admit that I am curious…" Her brows furrowed as she met Miranda's gaze and held it. "You could have evaded that binding charm if you wanted. Easily, I might add. Since it was my creation, I don't admit that lightly—"

"No! A witch couldn't break that spell, and that is what I am. Nothing else."

"But you do know what you are capable of," Peony surmised. "With blood like yours, I'm sure you are capable of things we can't even imagine—"

"No!" Miranda lurched to her feet, knocking over her mug in the process. "I do not do *that*," she spat. "Not willingly. Not ever."

"I understand," Peony said softly. "Apologies if I offended you. I thought you interesting before, but now I must admit that I am curious. Very curious. One day you will tell me your origins."

Miranda said nothing, unsure if a refusal would even matter. Something told her that Peony always got her way. But some stories weren't worth retelling, no matter the cost.

"Bargain or not, we don't know what the source of the magic is," she said, changing the subject to its original topic.

Peony stood and headed for the cauldron. "Well, then I suppose it's time we find out. Do bring that trunk," she called back. "We will need it."

TWENTY-FOUR

Damn Miranda Lightwood. Their bargain should have smothered any urge to think of her. He had gotten what he wanted—free access to her blood for as long as she remained in his orbit. Feeding from her was all that should have appealed to him, nothing more. And, though her taste lingered on his tongue, so did her moans echo ceaselessly in his mind.

Even if he killed her now, it wouldn't be soon enough.

Waiting for her to fulfill her end of their bargain was somehow worse than enduring the most gruesome battles he could remember. War was predictable, if bloody. The outcome was clear.

This… Toying with a witch once had nearly cost him everything in the end. So why was a part of him so damn eager to take all he could from this one before she had the chance to betray him?

Fortifying the manor should have been his sole focus. He met with Benjamin and increased patrols in and out of the house, as well as posted guards beside every entrance. Despite the increased vigilance, they hadn't found so much as a stray hair, let alone any mystery intruder. So he doubled the manpower and told them to look again.

Rather than head out to patrol himself, he instead found his way to Peony's storeroom. Unsurprisingly, the mage wasn't alone.

He almost wished the wench had refused his offer. Locked in his dungeon, he could ignore her presence, but with her roaming freely...

Her smell drenched the air, flooding every space. There was no escape from her. Even her voice affected him, sinking beneath his skin. There was a musical quality to the dour notes when she spoke excitedly of her potions and magic. Despite the urgency, he found himself pausing to listen.

"...know what this means?" she exclaimed. "I can delve more into—"

"Into what?" A part of him craved to eavesdrop, but he couldn't deny the pleasure he got out of watching alarm dance across those stern features as she whirled to face him.

"A private matter," Peony interjected, her hands on her hips. "This magic business is hard work. I'm going to the garden to gather more supplies. We can continue this tomorrow, Miranda."

She left, and Atiernan felt a tendril of irritation at what she'd so casually revealed.

"Tomorrow," he echoed, turning his sole focus to the witch. "So it seems you aren't in a hurry to return to your coven."

She flinched, but Atiernan wasn't satisfied. Oh no. He craved to poke many more cracks in her façade. Mentally. Physically. Sexually…

"I must endure your presence for one more night," he murmured. "Unfortunately for you, I am responsible for keeping watch over the barriers. Do you know what that means?"

He waited, amused as she processed his words. In case she required clarity, he added, "That *means* I will require sustenance. Present your throat to me."

He almost regretted not feeding from her thigh again, but he would show her a small amount of mercy and rotate sites. Though, he really longed for nothing more than to drain her dry, heedless of the damage that might be caused.

The bloodlust came from nowhere, almost too strong to resist. Peony wasn't here to call him back—a fact that both alarmed and excited him. No witnesses. No guardrails either.

Only his conscience would keep him from going too far, and Miranda seemed determined to strain it to the limits.

He expected her to fight. To resist and jab that haughty chin into the air. Instead, she tilted her head, those eyes a questioning brown. "In here?"

Her tone was deceptively innocent. He knew better—someone like her wouldn't give a damn if blood got on Peony's floors. No. She was afraid of how she might react to him—not with fear and screams, but those gasping moans he relished hearing again.

Something primal stirred within him, and he could barely choke out a coherent reply. "No. Come."

He entered the hall, painfully aware of her delicate footsteps echoing in his wake. Where exactly was he headed? He had no idea, though he wasn't surprised when his steps finally slowed near a room on the top floor.

As Miranda crossed the threshold first, he observed her from behind. She was small, even for a witch, but her indignant confidence made up for her slight form. She carried herself with more self-importance than some of the most adept warriors he'd met in his day. As if she'd slain hundreds armed only with that pert little mouth.

But beneath that bravado was a vulnerability that called to him far more. She was fragile behind that smart tongue. The predator in him craved to know how, if only to exploit the knowledge. It was in his nature.

To dominate and devour.

"Lie on the bed and wait for me," he commanded, though he didn't turn to see if she obeyed. He wished she wouldn't. It would give him all the reason to react impulsively without thinking thoughts that puzzled him.

Mainly...

"You fear the dark," he said, voicing a topic at random. "Why? I could sense it when I fed from you before. Fear, but not of me."

A fear that he glimpsed whenever he threatened to close the door to her cell completely.

She scoffed, but from the direction of the sound, he knew she had done as commanded. Why that aggravated him further? He didn't know.

"I promised you blood, daemon. Nothing else."

"You will tell me." He didn't mean it quite as a threat. More so a warning. "Captives are not entitled to secrets."

"Then I suggest you reshape our bargain, daemon," the witch replied.

He turned to find that, as expected, she'd partially obeyed his request—she was seated on the edge of the mattress, her hands neatly arranged on her lap. He saw through the pious gesture, though—her fingers trembled, and she was desperate to hide that from him. What else was she desperate to hide?

He swept his gaze over her, homing in on the pallor to her skin and the slight quiver in her throat. A million reasons could explain her unease, but he settled on just one.

"Peony told you about far more than potions, witch," he surmised.

To his surprise, she nodded. "She told me that you consorted with a witch. The one you mentioned. Liva."

He hissed through clenched teeth. Damn the mage, though he knew better than to take his irritation out on her. The woman quivering before him made for a far more appealing target. "What else did she tell you?"

Her hard swallow made him realize he'd taken a step toward her—not that he backed away. Instead, he leaned in, breathing in her tempting scent. Oddly enough, he couldn't decipher any fear. Just...

Deception.

"Nothing," she rasped, but her eyes darted away from him.

"I think you're lying to me, witch. In fact, we *will* restructure our bargain—"

"Good." Her sudden eagerness unnerved him. She smoothed her hands along the skirt of her dress, one most likely borrowed from Peony, given the drab color. He hated to admit that pink suited her far better. "I want to know more about my coven, and the witch you claim founded it."

"I don't think you understand the price of what you're asking for," Atiernan warned softly. "More than blood. Higher, I think, than you are willing to pay."

"No." She raised an eyebrow, her voice surprisingly strong. "You underestimate me, daemon. I am willing to pay any price."

He laughed, amused enough to humor her. "And if I asked for you to turn over your coven to me? To expose your close-held witch secrets? To offer up the blood of every mortal friend, lover, and accomplice you've ever known? Will you honor those requests?"

She paled, but didn't flinch. "No. I will, however, offer you anything pertaining solely to me."

He waited for her to temper that statement with a caveat. To blush and politely decline anything involving her body as well. He waited.

She didn't say a damn word.

"And if I asked you to fuck me and every man here every day and night from now until the second I let you crawl back to your coven?"

Her throat jerked around a swallow, but it was nowhere close to the horrified reaction he craved. "I would expect it," she admitted hoarsely. "But I would endure. Is that your price?"

"No." It was his turn to sound breathless. He approached her, unable to keep from reaching out. His hand captured her throat—a column so slender, he would only need one hand to strangle the life from her. Without conscious thought, his thumb traced the throbbing pulse point just beneath the tender skin.

He would drain her dry, first. Though she seemed to recover quickly, for a witch.

Already, her wounds were scabbing over and seemed to cause her little pain. Odd. Daemons could heal quickly with the proper treatment, but he wouldn't expect such rapid improvement in a witch. The fact bothered him, though another concern quickly wormed into his brain to supplant it. Her pulse fluttered against his fingertips.

Oh, how sweet her blood would be if he ripped that vessel wide open and let it drain.

"Do you realize what I've just implied?" he heard himself tell her. "You are brave, witch. Not foolish. I suggest you tailor your boast."

Because like hell would he ever share her.

She would belong solely to him. Her blood. Her body. Her soul.

"I would endure," she said, her gaze fixed on the wall beyond him. "No matter what evil you have in store for me, daemon. As long as you uphold your end of our bargain."

"And if I refuse?" He withdrew his hand, ignoring how his fingers twitched, aching to touch her again. "To arm a witch with the knowledge of a dangerous, deceitful ancestor. Hmm. That seems mighty foolish to me."

She turned to him, an eyebrow raised. "Are you saying that you are afraid of me?"

Atiernan didn't know how to read that sly, faint gleam in her eyes. It wasn't the greedy glint he'd come to recognize within Liva's. No... Hungrier. As if she had no choice but to feed on whatever glimmers of the past he'd fed her. She was starving for knowledge.

But to what aim?

"I've already fed from you more than once," he pointed out, his voice harsher. "You think your coven will so eagerly accept you again? And if I do more to damage and use that beautiful little body? They will shun you."

She winced as if he'd struck her—at least one of those jabs hit their mark.

But not for the reason he thought.

"You think I am afraid of being *tainted*?" He'd never heard her quite this scornful. It deepened her voice, adding a viciousness to it he wouldn't expect from her kind. "I'm not. Do your worst. As long as I live, I will survive it."

"Then tell me why you fear the dark."

This again. He didn't know why that one weakness of hers appealed to him so much. Perhaps because it was the easiest to exploit? And perhaps because he already knew the answer.

Mortals and witches alike feared what they could not easily understand. Even with torchlight, electricity, or a million different forms of illumination, you could only expose so much of the darkness. Shadows would always remain.

"Even children fear the dark," she croaked, proving his point. "There isn't a particular reason."

And yet…

"You're lying." He marveled at how sloppily she did so, as if she wasn't used to speaking in the necessary cadence required to lie convincingly. He shied away from the idea before it could fully form. No. Witches were bred in lies and deceit. Obviously, this was a trick. To what aim?

"Do you fear the daemons your old crones warned might be lurking in the shadows?"

He touched her again, boldly stroking a finger from the base of her throat, up to that delicate jawline. To his alarm, she endured the contact without flinching—though he knew she wanted to.

"How apt that you accuse me of lying," she said, eyeing the wall once more.

He couldn't keep his nail from pressing slightly into her flesh. Enough to watch her squirm. "Do explain your insult, witch," he scolded. "No vague slights here."

"Fine." She craned her neck back, finding his gaze. "Falsehoods come to you so easily that you don't even realize when you've spoken them," she countered, her eyes sparkling with that triumphant confidence. "Did you not even realize? You called me beautiful."

"You *are* beautiful." The words came to him so easily—no one could doubt his sincerity.

Not even her.

Though, objectively, a part of him argued that she had a point. In no way would she ever compare to Liva. She didn't have to. Beauty was measured in far more than physical attributes. Unfortunately, she made up for what she lacked in plenty of ways he hated to acknowledge.

Her lips parted. She was in such a hurry to refute him, she could barely spit out her words coherently. "False flattery is a *lie*—"

"You have clear skin." His voice deepened as he traced a sliver of it for himself, relishing the taut feel. "Your body is shapely enough. Your lips are…"

Too damn full, quivering with confusion. For once, she didn't have an argument at the ready, and her silence alone tempted him to continue despite his common sense.

"The sounds you make when you feel pleasure. Your fragile excuse for bravery, even now. Don't tell me you witches are shallow enough to relegate beauty only to the obvious."

She swallowed. Again and again. "Don't… Compliments get you nowhere, daemon—"

"I don't have time for compliments." He dismissed her with a cold laugh but continued to explore that soft jawline, down to the corner of that plump, sweet mouth. "I am honest. Honest, in a way that makes you uncomfortable, I can tell. You are used to having your appearance used against you."

It was more than that. She was so damn defensive when it came to any sort of praise. He'd noticed it even while she'd been around Peony. For a second, he wondered what kind of upbringing could have led to such a mindset. Had her parents been too demanding? Too strict?

"I am honest enough to tell you directly that I find aspects of you attractive, but you can't even be honest with yourself," he said instead.

Her eyes were darting again, avoiding him. He could almost read her mind, knowing the fear that weighed on it.

"You think I'm going to bite you," he announced, returning his touch to her exposed throat. "But you aren't afraid. No. Deep down, some rebellious part of you wants to feel my fangs piercing your flesh, witch."

"Never!" She recoiled, slapping his hand away.

For whatever reason, he didn't react the way he should have —by retaliating viciously enough to deter her from ever striking him again. She was still dangerous, fully armed with her power.

And yet. He wasn't alarmed by the prospect of her hurting him.

"You hate that you can enjoy what I've done to you," he said, watching how she flinched, her eyes on the floor. "You hate acknowledging that pleasure. The prospect of rape or abuse doesn't scare you. It relieves you. Such pain can make it easier to hate what was done to you. Fear me. Keep that resolve of yours intact. I suspect you desperately crave to cling to your resolve, Miranda."

Her eyes widened, but still, she brandished that chin. "So then do your worst, daemon. I am not afraid."

"You aren't," he admitted. "Not of me. You fear yourself."

He advanced, but she didn't cower or cringe in fear. Not until he cupped one of the small breasts shaping the front of her gown. He made sure to keep the contact light, allowing her every chance to pull away. Resist.

Which she did with a visible shudder.

"You hate that you can enjoy my touch should you let yourself. You hate knowing how tempting it is to give in. Give up. You fear your own pleasure, don't you? That resolve is all you have left."

His taunt resonated far deeper than it should have. Her eyes widened, her lower lip caught between her teeth. She bit down, hard enough to draw a bead of blood that made his vision go red.

"*That* is what I want from you," he rasped, clinging to a small shred of self-control. "That pleasure. I want you to admit it here and now—you liked when I fed from you. Say it."

Her expression hardened, her eyes glazing over. It was as if the smart-mouthed witch retreated behind a mask, leaving a shell of the woman behind.

"That is my price," he told her, unable to keep his voice steady. It alarmed him just how badly he wanted it—to have her moan unbidden. Tell him the truth. Drop the act and let him in. "For that, I will give you whatever you want to know."

The promise of knowledge alone was what made her blink and shirk her mask. She faced him again, her gaze wary.

"You want me to lie," she told him, voice rasping. "That's all it would be. A lie. An act. But I can give you that fantasy."

"Tell me that you enjoyed it when I fed from you," he countered. Lie or not, a part of him wanted to hear her say it, word for word.

"I…" Panic transformed her features. That was a step too far.

No worry. He'd had millennia to hone his patience.

"Something simpler, then," he suggested. "Tell me why you really fear the dark."

She shook her head so imperceptibly he wondered if she realized she'd done it.

"No?" He laughed coldly. "There is a part of our dungeon I have yet to show you, witch. You think your cell is unbearable? We have a crypt, not far from it. There are stone tombs we once used to trap a witch far more cunning than you. You fear darkness? Well, you haven't known isolation until you're buried beneath inches of stone so thick that no one can hear your screams. Perhaps that should be your new quarters?"

More panic flashed in her eyes, but she was able to swallow it down, he noted. Licking her lips, she met his gaze again.

"My mother would lock me in our cellar if I failed to perform a spell properly..."

She didn't expect to share that with him. He could see her horror. Her confusion.

And damn. It tasted sweeter than any blood.

"Go on."

She shook her head.

"I will tell you more of Liva," he said, baiting the hook. He was as surprised with himself as she seemed to be. Those memories were long since buried. It wouldn't do good to retread them, not for anything.

Except for the promise of more truth from her. She made him reckless enough to gamble his own sanity. For what?

Tales from a witch about a strict upbringing? No. There was more to it. Something that made her shiver, and her chest heave. Something that made those eyes glisten with unshed tears. He was growing accustomed to her pleasure, but this was pain. A taste of her true agony.

And he needed more of both to properly compare the two.

"Give me more."

"She... She would put me in the dark," she croaked, wringing her slim fingers together. "Until I did the spell properly. If I failed, I stayed there."

"How long?" He didn't mean in general. He meant the source behind her horror and fear. The time frame that haunted her nightmares. He wanted that.

"Days," she rasped, staring blankly.

It wasn't a lie, and yet... He sensed it wasn't the whole truth, either. This was the story she told herself to avoid the real horror behind her fear. He knew firsthand how such a trick came in handy. After all, he fed himself pathetic half-truths when it came to Liva, if only to avoid the true wealth of despair her name inspired.

An ache panged in his chest that he didn't recognize. Pity?

Her upper lip curled as if she could smell it in him. That alone was enough to erase the vulnerability and make her hard again.

"Don't look so shocked, daemon," she hissed. "As if one poor witch had an upbringing so different from yours."

She seemed so smug, but this was one arena in which Atiernan had no problem taking her on directly.

"No witch," he said. "My mother never locked me in a room until I fulfilled a task. She never harmed me. Not even once."

He'd forgotten most of his childhood—it was so long ago. Only traces remained, but he cherished them all. Enough to say for certain that the woman who raised him would have never done such a thing.

"Never would Peony do that to her daughter," he added out loud. "What else did she do to you?"

"As if the daemons are the pinnacle of parenthood."

"Ah, but that's where you are wrong," Atiernan replied. "Peony is more of a mother than you or any other witch could ever hope to be. Were you a child of hers, she would have stormed this fortress and burned it to the ground to get you back. Nothing and no one would stop her."

"Is she your mother?" the witch asked. He couldn't tell if she was being mocking.

Not that he cared.

"Yes," he said heatedly. "She didn't give birth to me, but she is my mother in every other sense of the word. Too many years ago for you to fathom, witch, she took me in when she had nothing and raised me alongside her own child. Never, not once, did she ever treat me any differently or make me feel like a burden. Never would she lock me away for the hell of it. Insult her in front of me, and you will regret it."

"Spare me your theatrics," the witch spat. "I want to know the terms of your bargain. State them now so we can end this game."

"My terms?" He watched her, marveling at just how much effort she put into maintaining her charade. It had to be exhausting—still, she put on a good show, chin in the air, eyes blazing. He blamed curiosity for the words that sprung from his lips next. "I want you to be honest with me,

Miranda. In every sense of the word. Physically. Mentally. You keep nothing from me."

Her eyes clouded over again, and he imagined her puzzling over how to deceive him, but still uphold her end of the bargain. Whatever knowledge she sought, she considered it worth her pride. But her soul?

"I have been honest with you from the start," she hissed. "But fine. I will humor that request—"

"Is that so?"

"But I want something first," she said breathlessly. "Your witch. Liva. You claimed she did blood magic, but how? Blood magic requires daemon blood. Was... Was she part daemon?"

He frowned. "As if a hybrid of our races is even possible," he replied, openly mocking her. Bethaem was only part human, and Peony nearly died bringing her into the world. A half-witch would have been a step too far, even if the creature survived its birth.

Not even Liva was *that* corrupted.

Miranda looked rightly disgusted. "But then how?"

"No, witch. Liva used the blood of a daemon. Mine. I gave her my blood willingly, and the bitch nearly bled me dry. That was how she performed her twisted magic."

He didn't stop to see how Miranda reacted to that truth. He turned, leaving her there despite every primal urge in his body demanding he go back and drink.

She'd offered herself to him, after all.

For once, his pride was stronger. She thought him a brute and a monster? Well, he would let her reconcile with the fact that most of her upbringing had been based on a lie.

"That is something they won't tell you in your precious history books. Your founding witch dabbled in blood magic derived from the blood of a daemon. Her daemon lover, in fact. Your coven and your sacred lands were achieved through that which you consider the most taboo. Does that bother you, witch?"

He looked back at her then, but rather than horrified, she just looked resigned. As if nothing he'd told her shocked her in the least. If anything...

It saddened her, but not in the way he thought. She wasn't devastated, just disappointed. Wounded.

As if something he'd said had hurt her personally, far more than he would ever know.

Confusion was almost enough to make him return to her. Almost. The way her eyes cut in his direction kept him back.

"Go," he told her. "I won't feed from you tonight."

"But—"

"Our bargain is still intact," he said harshly. "But know this —I didn't mince words. You give me everything. Your blood. Your body. You offer it willingly, and you won't hide behind fear and hate. When I sink my fangs into your throat, you moan the way you've stopped yourself from doing. Do you understand?"

He didn't care if she replied to him or not.

He already knew her answer—it would kill her to abide by his rules. Destroy her.

But she would have no choice.

It was in her blood. Witches were spiteful creatures, but they were honorable to a fault.

And he would gladly take advantage of her honor to bring her to her knees.

CHAPTER
TWENTY-FIVE

Miranda couldn't keep the tears at bay any longer. The second she returned to her cell alone, they fell, streaming down her cheeks in burning rivulets.

Damn him. The daemon enjoyed toying with her, dangling her emotions on a string. To even insinuate that she had *enjoyed* what he did to her…

Insulting didn't begin to describe it. Humiliating. Disguising. *Truthful…* To the point that she couldn't even face herself in the mirror since the day he pierced her throat. Part of it was shame, but mostly confusion.

Shouldn't he, if anyone, be able to tell what she really was? He praised her sweet witch's blood, but Miranda was beginning to suspect he hadn't been mocking her. He truly believed her to be as pure as Peony claimed.

Yet, the mage had seen right through her. How long until Atiernan realized it as well?

Then he would parade her through his manor as an abomination.

Not that she would give him the chance to do so.

Once she was sure night fell, she crept from the dungeon and found her way to Peony's storeroom. She was convinced Atiernan would have had dozens of his men assigned to watch her every move, but she passed no one but the usual guards who didn't spare her a second glance.

Perhaps the man didn't believe her to be a threat after all.

Or perhaps he knew she'd be foolish to try anything against him.

Though... Peony had insinuated surprise that she hadn't done so already by evading the binding spell. As if it would be so easy to circumvent honest magic.

It didn't matter what anyone claimed—she was a witch first and foremost. Witches drew their power from their mortal bodies and nature itself.

Nothing else.

Though, Peony had unknowingly given her all she needed to source a tracking spell of her own. If Atiernan had truly sired a bloodline he knew nothing of, that bloodline was also tethered to Liva, a witch.

Such hybrids were taboo—aberrations of the worst kind. Though, ironically, Miranda knew one positive of being such a creature—there weren't many, narrowing down her search considerably.

Rolling up her sleeves, she fetched the remnants of the spell she and Peony had brewed earlier. Aware of the seconds ticking by, she dipped her fingers in the salve and drew upon her power before Atiernan or anyone else could come looking for her.

The spell was simple in essence—she called out to every being within a nearby radius with cursed blood. All twisted, unholy, unnatural abominations. All things broken and sullied...

She anticipated her call would be met by the most grievous, heinous beasts imaginable.

But she didn't expect a lone voice to answer back in a language she understood.

Who are you?

She audibly gasped and barely kept her focus on the spell. The voice echoed inside her head, but as distinctly as if the speaker had spoken directly into her ear. He had a gruff voice. Soft, too. So unexpectedly nonhostile that she found herself responding.

Who are you?

She could imagine them laughing, but not in amusement. Disbelief?

You are a witch, they deduced. *But, frankly, I don't think you are who I hoped to speak with.*

Their politeness confused her further. It had been so long since anyone took pains to be so...cordial. Even Atiernan, for all his loathing of her, spoke to her with more respect than those in her coven did. A tendril of unease ran down her spine at the unintentional comparison—Peony's worst fears may have just been confirmed.

You are the man I saw. You sent the sentinel after Atiernan, she replied mentally. *Why?*

She didn't give them time to respond. Expanding her consciousness, she entered their mind without warning. It wasn't anywhere near as invasive as scrying, though insightful enough to give her a clearer view of who she spoke with. A man. His thoughts were foreign but oddly… normal. She glimpsed a sleepy town similar to the one outside of the forest where her coven dwelled. A battered pickup truck. A radio playing country music. A name. *Marcus.*

Don't—the warning accompanied a force that mentally propelled her back so firmly she staggered, barely able to stay upright.

If this man wanted to, he could have cut the connection then. But he didn't. Tentatively, his consciousness returned, brushing against hers.

You aren't just a witch, he replied wryly. *Otherwise, you couldn't maintain a spell like this from such a distance. To answer your question—I didn't send the monster. I wanted to help you defeat it, but I couldn't maintain my hold in that realm for long. My methods for traversing realms last minutes at most. You must be very powerful to reach me here.*

She startled at the insinuation. Was he truly in the mortal realm? But how could he travel from the two worlds so quickly?

Who are you? she tried again, though she felt bold enough to mention the name she'd gleaned. *Marcus?*

And you are Miranda, he replied. *Captive of the daemon Atiernan, still alive, which I am glad to see.*

She flinched, positive he hadn't invaded her mind in return. Which meant he'd known of her beforehand. How?

Why did you send the sentinel after him and his people? she asked.

I didn't, the man replied. *I was curious of the answer myself.*

How did you get into the manor?

Answer my question first, he replied. *What is a half-breed doing masquerading as a witch?*

Miranda felt her cheeks flame. *I am a witch,* she replied fiercely.

Suddenly, the energy she sensed shifted, becoming slightly less defensive. *I offended you. I am sorry. It's rare to meet someone like us.*

Us. The comparison made her want to retch.

I am nothing like you.

Another laugh. Then a sigh. *I am not behind the sentinel attacks, but I would like to meet Atiernan.*

Why?

Because he is my father.

Disbelief was her first impulse.

You are lying. Any child of his would be ancient—

I would like to speak to him, Marcus replied over her. *But not because of who he is. The sentinels are just the start.*

He would never believe me, Miranda replied.

Then I will help you prove that I mean no harm. The sentinels will attack again. I can tell you how to craft a weapon to defeat them.

How?

You know the answer. I wanted to speak to Atiernan directly, but I couldn't. You need daemon blood. Then you need to convince him to meet me. If not, it will be too late to stop it. Already, things have been set into motion.

His phrasing could be written off as overly dramatic to prove a point—but not his tone. He truly believed in the urgency of whatever he planned to prevent.

Warily, she took the bait. *Stop what?*

The end of the world. Now, unfortunately, I need to go. Should you convince Atiernan to meet me, you apparently know how to find me. Goodbye.

He withdrew so abruptly that Miranda gasped, sinking to her knees. Her head throbbed as the effects of the spell receded, but she couldn't move long after her senses returned.

Atiernan had a son—a witch hybrid. The implications were chilling. Though she hated the man, she realized how much he prided himself on providing safety for those in his care. A daemon hybrid capable of using blood magic could undo the wards protecting this place in an instant.

And send a horde of sentinels to finish the job.

But why now? Millennia after the child's supposed conception, why would Liva choose now to attack a man so reclusive he'd been relegated to a legend? It didn't make sense. And Marcus... Would he really choose now to enact a grudge against his father thousands of years in the making?

No. Miranda knew firsthand that those wounds reached a boiling point long before adulthood. She shivered at the memory and ran a hand along her right forearm. Even now, those scars were the most prominent among her collection. The most severe.

She'd ripped open those wounds with her teeth, blinded by rage and hate. Never again would she be so weak.

And never again would she ever resort to using blood magic herself.

She shook her head to banish the thought and headed into the hall, aiming to return to her cell. She'd barely taken a step over the threshold when a piercing sound shattered the silence. It was high-pitched like the droning of a bell that went on and on—an alarm.

Around her, the house came alive as the occupants streamed from various directions, shouting amongst themselves. From their chatter, she picked out one word that made her head for the dungeons. *Sentinel.*

She loathed facing one of those creatures again—or having Atiernan accuse her of allowing it inside. Her cell was the best possible place to be.

Though, it seemed the daemon lord was one step ahead of her. Already, he lurked near the mouth of the stairwell leading down below. His eyes were alight with an intensity that set her hair on end. Though, she could sense he was wary of her, but not openly hostile. Yet.

"It's a warning," he explained, inclining his head to indicate the piercing sound still ringing off the walls. "The sentinels have been spotted nearby, but they haven't breached the barriers just yet."

Sure enough, the sound fell silent, though the footsteps of the daemons continued, racing toward various directions.

"Women and children will retreat to the inner rooms for shelter while the men take up patrol," Atiernan explained.

"How archaic of you," Miranda snapped. She couldn't help the vitriol. Being near the man was strange when she knew so much he seemed oblivious to. Was this feeling guilt? It wormed beneath her skin, interfering with every breath she drew in.

His nearness unnerved her. It felt as though with every passing second, he would be able to sense her deception—if he hadn't already.

"You, however," he murmured, eyeing her throat. "You will stay with me until the creatures either breach the walls or retreat. In either case, you will not leave my sight. Do you understand?"

Focus, Miranda. She sucked in a breath and prepared herself to meet his gaze. She almost succeeded in conveying bravery. Almost. Until she glimpsed something in his eyes that wasn't hate or disgust.

It was hunger—but one not entirely regulated to food or blood. It was the way men used to glance at the most beautiful women in the coven during their gatherings. A way no one ever looked at her.

She recalled his confession from earlier. He found her beautiful. But how much of a compliment was that coming from someone like him—a beast who sowed gruesome wars and relished in the carnage. To him, death was beautiful.

Perhaps it was because of what she was that he found interest in her at all. Some primal, twisted part of him could sense her corruption. The same way any normal man instinctively knew to stay far away from her.

"Come." Atiernan frowned and beckoned her with a nod before he turned and headed down the hall. She was surprised that, rather than his study or the fortress walls, he led her to the large room she assumed to be his. At a glance, the space appeared far too plain to belong to someone revered as a lord. Her old room in her mother's house had more decoration.

In the form of the warding charms that caused her excruciating pain whenever she disobeyed.

"This changes things," Atiernan explained, supposedly his reasoning for bringing her here. It was more than keeping her close. The fangs protruding from beneath his upper lip cemented that fear. "If the sentinels are to attack, I need to be ready. Present your—"

She threw her head back before he could finish, almost eager to get this over with. The sooner the man grew tired of her, the sooner they could end their bargain—and hopefully with a new light wood tree gained by the end.

That was all. She wasn't eager to be used by him. No. For her people, she could endure anything.

"I never said where I wanted to feed from," Atiernan scolded.

Miranda lowered her chin enough to find him watching her intently without an ounce of amusement.

"Present your wrist," he said coldly. Then he sat on the end of the bed, his expression blank.

Miranda cleared her throat and approached him, extending her hand. He grabbed it, tugging her closer. She gasped, stumbling forward, and landing on his lap.

The daemon had the nerve to chuckle as she scrambled to compose herself. He felt so hard, unlike the few men she'd ever interacted with. They had wanted her for superficial reasons. For close proximity to her mother. For pure boredom mixed with lust.

No one ever conformed to her body the way his did. Like every breath she drew in, his chest expanded to steal. Her nipples scraped the inside of her tunic, overly sensitive as warmth teased her through the fabric.

His hands were so large—the one on her wrist felt like a manacle while the other came to steady her by the waist.

All of that she could have endured, though. All of it.

But the way he looked at her... His eyes were molten, holding her stare as if she fascinated him for reasons he couldn't explain. His fangs were extended, his lips glistening with hunger, but his gaze didn't leave hers in favor of a vein. It was as if he were taunting her to turn away first. Flinch in fear. Cower.

He wanted her fear.

She swallowed and squared her chin instead.

"You may drink, my lord." A part of her sneered at her breathless tone.

He, however, wasn't amused.

"I want my payment first," he told her in a voice that raised goosebumps. "Have you ever been with a man?"

Her cheeks flamed, and she flinched back. It took every ounce of pride she had to remain there, hunched against him. She knew damn well what he meant, and his polite phrasing irritated her further. Damn him.

"Fucking," he clarified when she said nothing. "Have you ever had a man inside of you?"

"Y-Yes," she rasped. "Plenty. Enough to never allow myself to be sullied by a daemon."

Lies. Lies. Lies. She'd slept with one man—an outsider who ran the second he learned her true nature. Everyone did in the end.

She'd gotten over it. A witch devoted to her coven required no one, man or otherwise. Ironically, her mother had taught her that much.

Still, the lie sounded convincing to her own ears. It should have fed his curiosity. Instead, those dark eyes glimmered unsettlingly.

"You were an outcast," he pointed out, and she stiffened at the reminder that he'd watched her long before abducting her. "I could believe it."

Her cheeks flamed. She couldn't resist the bait. "What is that supposed to mean, daemon?"

He adjusted his grip on her wrist to raise the limb for his inspection. Words couldn't explain the emotions running through her as he inspected the bluish veins visible beneath her skin.

"It means that an outcast would have few options, though fewer reasons to refuse any suitor. You've either had several men or none at all. Though, I believe you think you've experienced enough. You don't strike me as the seductress type."

"And why is that?"

His upper lip quirked into a chilling smirk. "You would have tried to seduce me."

"Whore or not, I would never be desperate enough for a daemon," Miranda spat.

Or ambitious enough. Her mother hadn't sought a lover when she struck a deal with the figurative devil. Just power, no matter the cost.

Sometimes, she wondered if the old crone regretted her deal in the end. Though, perhaps her regret was enough for them both. Never would she do the same. Ever.

"You already were desperate enough," Atiernan pointed out. "You promised me your body. Everything but your soul, witch."

"I don't have a soul," she replied.

"Everything has a soul," Atiernan countered. "Even if it's been bruised and battered. You were tortured."

Miranda blinked. "I don't know what you mean," she began, but then she noticed where his gaze was.

On her forearm. She moved to cover the skin, but one look from him froze her in place.

"What made these marks?" he asked, releasing her wrist to stroke one jagged scar. "Not a knife. Not any weapon I recognize."

Miranda felt her lungs constrict—it was a struggle to suck in enough air.

"They're nothing," she rasped.

"I said no *weapon* could have made these marks, but I can guess what did—teeth," he said, and two of his peeked beneath his upper lip, lethally sharp. "The same pair of teeth, over and over, through years. Changing with age and strength. Yours?"

She was suffocating. All of the blood in her body surged to her skull, making her head feel weightless. A part of her feared it might detach from her body and float away.

As if escape would be that easy. His gaze was an anchor, freezing her in place no matter what.

"Answer me."

"I...It's nothing."

"These..." He dragged his thumb over a patch of roughened skin, shiny with thickened scars. "Nails. Human, or a witch's. Digging. Tearing. Answer me."

"I..."

"You hurt yourself." The pity in his voice. The disgust. The...rage?

No. She couldn't bear his sympathy. Anything but that.

"I had no choice," she snapped.

Too late did she realize what she'd implied.

His eyes narrowed to slits, and she shivered. This was a mere glimpse of the warrior lurking beneath the façade. A man who could bring armies to their knees.

And make her answer whatever questions he desired to ask.

"Someone forced you to harm yourself."

His tone was deadly soft, twisting her belly into knots.

"Speak!"

"You should drink, my lord," she croaked, twitching her extended limb. "In case the sentinels attack."

He opened his mouth slowly, exposing his teeth. Then he lowered his head and bit.

She should have been fully prepared for the sensation of his fangs sinking deep. For the way his lips settled over her flesh and his tongue...

Her eyelids fluttered as a sensation of fire washed through her veins. He asked her once if she enjoyed the feeling. She didn't.

She couldn't.

The taking of blood in any manner was an act meant to be abhorred. Feared. Loathed. And yet...

The bite of his fangs didn't feel anywhere near as painful as other methods she'd experienced. She knew pain better than most. She knew agony.

"Look at me."

Her heartbeat hammered through her ears as she opened her eyes to find Atiernan watching her, his lips painted red.

"Tell me what you feel," he demanded, his voice like sin.

She shook her head, too dazed to form a coherent response. "Not... Good."

"You're lying, witch." He chuckled, tugging her closer while spinning her around.

The hardness of his chest met her back as her hips settled over his thighs. Dangerously warm, his breath teased the side of her throat. "I wanted your honesty. Unless you've reneged on our agreement?"

Miranda eyed the marks left on her arm—two surprisingly delicate holes.

"It felt like a monster was feeding from me," she croaked.

"Liar." His laughter was harsher, edged with a hint of mocking. "You fear pain..." He dragged a finger over the line of a vein, making her shudder. Somehow, his skin gleamed like gold, reducing her to a pale shadow in comparison. Beside him, *she* looked more like a daemon. "I can tell. You tense every time I touch you, bracing for agony. But when I bite down, you relax, witch. I can taste the difference."

Her breath caught at the insinuation. "I relax because I have learned to endure even the worst torture, daemon."

Too late did she realize what that statement gave away.

"As suspected, you are used to pain," he remarked, but his voice was softer. "What could a witch who, until now, has lived safely within her coven experience to harden her so?"

Her initial impulse was to shut down. Deny him even a sliver of emotion to feed off of. Then she remembered what she promised him. Honesty.

He never, however, specified how much of it she was required to give him.

"Witches can be as cruel as daemons. Though, I'm sure you know that personally, given your history."

What she meant as a pointed jab at his expense resonated far differently when he sighed.

"Yes," he said hoarsely. "I know firsthand how cruel your kind can be. But these scars? They were self-inflicted."

She wrenched her hand away and tried to disguise the motion by smoothing her skirt. "Have you gotten your fill, my lord?"

"Don't evade the question I'm asking you," he warned, seizing her forearm so that she had no choice but to offer it to him. "Tell me. You hurt yourself. Why?"

"Does there need to be a reason?" she bit back.

But there was. One she would rather die than confess to him. Though, doing so would risk her retrieval of a light wood tree. Was that worth her pride?

No.

"Fine." Abruptly Atiernan sat back, allowing her to scramble off his lap. Then he stood. "Have it your way. Consider our bargain forfeit, witch—"

"I had to," she rasped, clutching her arm to her chest. "When I... It was the only way to make the pain stop."

"Pain from what?" He was closer than before, and he sounded almost concerned. A weaker woman might have fallen for the sudden dip in his inflection. Not her.

"From the darkness," she admitted. "Hurting myself was the only way to make the darkness stop."

"Someone did that to you."

She frowned, surprised by how her eyes burned. She blinked to dispel the sensation, and moisture fell in response. Tears? No. Just a trick of the light—it was far too bright in here.

"They locked you away until you hurt yourself," Atiernan said, displaying far more intelligence than she was comfortable giving him credit for. "Why?"

"Because..." She fixed her gaze on the far wall and desperately fished for the right wording. In the end, she decided that the truth was unbelievable enough to escape scrutiny. "Like all children, I disobeyed," she said. "I was punished. It is nothing more than that."

But he wasn't satisfied. Not by a long shot—and that puzzled her. His concern for a minor discomfort that probably paled in comparison to anything he'd experienced confounded her beyond reason.

"Miranda—"

Suddenly, another shrill alarm pierced the quiet. With a startled grunt, Atiernan inclined his head.

"There's been a breach," he said gruffly. "Stay here. I'll lock the door so that I know for certain you aren't anywhere near—"

"Wait." She licked her lips, weighing her words. There wasn't time for doubt. If her plan succeeded, she could be back in Hazel's Way by daybreak. "Do you think you can capture one of those creatures alive?"

Atiernan frowned. "At the risk of losing one of my men or more. Why?"

"If you can, I might be able to devise a weapon that can kill the beasts, but I will need a living subject to study first. It won't matter how many come if you have an effective way to defeat them."

He watched her, then headed for the doorway. "Stay here," he warned. "You only answer the door for me."

As he left, Miranda weighed the consequences of disobeying his order and finding her own way to get a sample from one of the creatures.

More than her life hinged on it.

Her very soul did as well.

TWENTY-SIX

A tiernan raced to the lower level, anxious to fight, even against a sentinel. He longed to do *something* other than dwell on the witch in his chambers.

She confounded him in the worst way, so damn coy one minute. Ice the next.

And yet, he didn't question her determination to uphold their agreement. She wanted that damn tree. Witches were puzzling creatures—it wasn't his place to wonder why.

He did anyway.

"Sir!" Benjamin rushed to meet him as he entered the great hall. "One creature breached the outer wall. We managed to contain the fallout for now—"

"Is it still alive?" he asked.

Benjamin raised an eyebrow. "The men are in the process of dispatching it now. They might be finished before we join them."

"Then let's go," Atiernan said grimly. "And hope we can beat them to it."

***

HE LINGERED OUTSIDE HIS CHAMBER, able to sense her heartbeat through the wooden door. She had obeyed him by staying here, not that she had very many places to go otherwise.

Still. The fact made his cock stiffen, and it was harder to focus on his true reason for confronting her now. Opening the door, he tossed an object held in his hand into the center of the room. It splattered with a sick thud, startling the witch from her seated position on the edge of his bed.

"The beast is alive," he said gruffly. "Should this be enough for you to complete your spells, witch?"

Her face paled as she realized just what he'd offered her—a chunk of flesh, still leaking a puddle of black blood. Just enough that the creature would survive locked within his dungeon for a few days at least. Though, that meant he suddenly had far less space there in which to store a captive witch.

"Y-Yes," she croaked, pressing a slim hand against her nose. "It should be enough."

"Good. One of my men will take it to Peony's storeroom. Now come."

He saw her draw in a quick breath, steeling herself the way she did whenever he brought her to her cell. Despite her apprehension, that haughty chin remained in the air as her footsteps echoed his.

In the end, they didn't go far. He opened the door beside his, revealing a room a maid was still in the process of preparing. Spotting him, the woman nodded respectfully and finished smoothing a set of white sheets over the bed. Then she left.

"My dungeon is full," Atiernan explained, aware of the witch lurking in the doorway. "You will stay here from now on."

"Here?" She crept past him, heading directly for the one fixture he suspected she'd be drawn to—a large window overlooking a section of forest. Her fingers brushed the glass reverently before she seemed to remember his presence. "I'm surprised you don't have a spare cage for every witch you capture."

"No," he countered, pleased to hear her heart flutter in response to his low tone. "You are far too dangerous to risk leaving out of my sight. Here is where you belong, where I can keep an eye on you myself."

She stiffened, and he suspected she realized how close her chamber was to his. Very—connected by a door just paces away. He didn't feel the need to point that out to her just yet. Instead, he watched her, letting his gaze rake over those slender limbs.

The sleeves of her dress were too short to cover her forearms completely. Still, she kept her arms angled away from him, hands clasped before her waist. Those injuries puzzled him, gnawing at the back of his mind. She didn't like when he brought attention to them. Whatever their true source, she was protective of it, enough to jeopardize the one thing she seemed to desire above all else.

"This tree," he said, prompting her to face him. "Why is it so important to you?"

He expected a superficial reason. Witches were so damn cunning, so hungry for power.

Sure enough, her eyes widened, betraying a ravenous appetite—but apparently not for power. "That tree is important to my coven," she explained heatedly. "For decades, we've strived to find another. If I could restore one to our sacred lands… It would mean much for future generations."

"You said the last one was destroyed?" He hadn't bothered to delve into that part of her tale earlier, but something in how she flinched instantly drew his notice.

"Yes. Years ago."

"How?"

Her gaze skittered away from his, settling on the nearby wall. "It was… burned."

From her fearful whisper, he assumed the fire wasn't caused intentionally. "By magic?"

She shrugged. "Nature provides us with everything vital. Who are we to question why and when it takes something away?"

There was more to it. She kept her face angled from his for a reason. The longer he spent near her, the easier it became to sense her deception. Contrary to every stereotype he harbored regarding witches, she thwarted his closely held beliefs. Miranda Lightwood was a terrible liar. She had no practice with it, no finesse with her words.

It didn't square with the other witches he'd known. She was different—and that unsettled him.

He advanced a step, coming up behind her. From this angle, he caught their image reflected in the window's glass. She was so small against him, frightfully pale.

"Am I to believe that, rather than power or money, you crave this tree merely for the glory of restoring it to your coven?"

He wanted to laugh just to highlight how obscured he found that idea.

"Yes!" She whirled to face him, and the intensity in her gaze caught him off guard. She was a bad liar, but shamelessly transparent when it came to what she truly desired. "Money and power are fleeting. Honor and legacy—those are forever."

"You wish to have a legacy?"

She blinked as if realizing how much of herself she'd given away with that one statement. Abruptly, she turned her back to him, facing the window, her spine rigid.

"I wish to survive my ordeal as a daemon's captive in one piece."

"I take it that you haven't interacted much with daemons." It was an obvious statement. He merely wanted to see her reaction, and she didn't disappoint. That haughty chin jutted higher, her jawline stone.

"Of course, I haven't. Daemons are banned from our sacred grounds, and only the most trusted in our coven are allowed to leave. Your kind are a blight on the natural world. Should I return to Hazel's Way, it will take days of prayer and incense to make me clean again."

"You were never clean." He meant it metaphorically. How high and mighty these witches had become—banishing him from the very land he helped Liva scout and protect.

Miranda interpreted his statement far differently. She gasped, her lips parting in horror. As if he'd issued the most grievous insult. Which shouldn't have mattered.

So why the hell did he care?

Suddenly, she lurched back, pressing her back to the window's glass. Only as her panicked breaths fanned his chest did he realize he'd approached her. Rather than retreat, he stood his ground, watching the witch scramble to accommodate his nearness—she seemed to hold her breath, just to keep her chest from contacting his. Without warning, he cupped her chin against his palm, running his thumb along the pulse thrumming in her throat. "I'm sorry—"

"Your words don't hurt me, daemon," she spat, evading his touch. "You know nothing about me. An insult from you means nothing."

"You're lying." That puzzled him more, drawing him nearer as she tried to scuttle away. He caught her wrist, easily pulling her toward him. "You've heard those words before," he deduced. "From someone you value far more than me."

"Stop your prattling!" She tugged at her wrist, and he imagined she'd slap her hands over her ears if she had the ability.

"I'm sorry if I hurt you. I am."

How many years had it been since he'd said those words to an outsider? Far too long to count.

From her reaction, one might think he'd just cursed the witch to hell and back. She panted, frowning at the wall, her chest heaving.

Atiernan wasn't insulted, but intrigued. The anomalies were adding up, painting a picture that contradicted everything she tried so hard to convey. A poor liar, unused to a compliment. So unaccustomed to an apology, she blushed at one issued by a daemon.

Damn her. It was her unusualness that made him second-guess every defensive guard he'd built up after Liva. If she were a beautiful, cunning, confident witch, he'd have no problem resisting her.

But Miranda... Her vulnerability was fleeting but irresistible to the part of him that craved a good hunt. And a willing victim.

"Look at me, witch," he commanded, his voice rougher than intended. "And tell me what really happened to your sacred tree—"

"You're bleeding." Her quiet observation threw him off, and he followed the line of her gaze to his chest. While subduing the sentinel, the bastard caught him with a claw. He'd live, and luckily the wound didn't seem likely to fester.

While his body was safe, his expectations seemed on the verge of being subverted by the witch yet again. For once, Miranda's eyes blazed with confidence, betraying a familiarity with violence. And blood.

"Will you heal me, witch?" he asked, fully expecting a nasty refusal.

Instead, she tilted her head, scrutinizing the wound. "It's superficial. You won't need a potion."

Lost in her sudden role of healer, she approached him on her own, reaching out without warning. She pressed her hand to his chest, and he had to silence a groan. She could be so damn gentle when she wanted to be. The skin on her fingertips was akin to silk. He almost feared his scarred, damaged flesh would be too rough in contrast.

"You aim to use your power on me, witch?" he grated as she settled her fingers along a tear in his shirt, near his wound.

Closing her eyes, she ignored him, her lips moving silently. A telltale prickle of heat warned that, indeed, she had drawn upon her power. Not to hurt, but to encourage the edges of his wound to meet and for the skin to seal as if never injured.

This wasn't his first time being subjected to such power. There was a brief stretch of history when Liva would heal him daily, using her hands much in the way this witch was, millennia later.

But there was a distinct difference. Magic, to Liva, had been a game. She used her spells frivolously, almost carelessly. But Miranda...

Her brows were furrowed in deep concentration. Though she made no secret about loathing his kind, her touch was soft. Delicate. When she finally withdrew, he grunted in alarm at the sensation.

"You are very skilled." It sounded like a compliment, but it was yet another reason why he should have been on guard around her. "Thank you."

Her cheeks flushed, and she pursed her lips into a thin line, unamused by his praise.

"Do you daemons even feel pain?" she sniped. "As long as you've lived, this was nothing but a scratch to you."

"I feel many things," he said, taking a step toward her.

Her eyes widened as her throat contorted around a hard swallow. He'd unnerved her. Good.

"Pain. Anger. Hatred," he went on huskily. "Lust... If you look at me, I'm sure it's obvious what I'm feeling now."

Too much lust. Damn. Her magic must have worked on him in more ways than one. His erection strained the front of his trousers, but every new intake of her scent just hardened him more. Damn. He hadn't felt desire like this since...

No, even Liva hadn't affected him in this way. There was something about *her*—Miranda. She made him want to break his unofficial celibacy for the first time in several thousand years.

"Look at me," he commanded as she stubbornly eyed the wall behind him.

Warily, her gaze flickered in his direction but avoided direct eye contact. No worry. He contented himself with watching her in return, trying to decipher what about her called to him so. Not her beauty. Though hell, on second appraisal, he couldn't find any fault with her simple, but striking features. She was much like a gem taken from a mine, coated in dirt and dust. When viewed in the right conditions, however, the various facets caught the light. An observer was riveted. Enthralled.

And removing the layers shrouding the stone only exposed more of its beauty.

He said nothing as he reached for her chin, capturing it against his palm. He moved closer, forcing her to crane her neck to finally meet his gaze. He knew from how her eyes widened that she could see his intentions.

She knew damn well what he intended even before he lowered his lips to hers.

And yet, she didn't pull away.

He planned to sample her—just a taste of what those plump lips could offer. Nothing more. He fully expected her to recoil in disgust, anyway. But, by the gods, she was so damn soft. So warm. So…still. Impulsively, he prodded her lower lip with his tongue, stealing inside.

And he found Hell. Not the fiery landscape wrought with torture that humans imagined—just the alien realm itself. Something different from the usual. A feral, vicious space and yet one with an appeal he couldn't deny.

He pulled her closer, crushing her to his chest. At the same time, he deepened the kiss, probing harder, taking more. More.

It was never enough.

As a Raeth, he'd lived under the grim knowledge that bloodlust couldn't be rivaled by any other impulse. Not lust. Not love. Even Peony struggled to reach him when he was under its sway, and he respected her above all others.

Until now, no other torment ever came close to hunger. In this moment, he craved more than the witch's blood. More than her tempting heat, or even the cleft awaiting between her legs. Her entire body seemed to fuel some unnatural, vicious craving that grew in intensity with every passing second. He could feel her breath on his face, and hear her pulse hammering like mad. Her lips parted against his in shock.

And that alone was enough to tip him over the edge.

He shoved her back, mounting her as she fell against the mattress. Idiot, he scolded himself once he spotted the healing wound on her neck. To his relief, she didn't appear to be in pain, and the stitches remained intact, even as she swallowed hard and ran a pink tongue along her lower lip.

Atiernan's mind went blank at the sight—those lips recalled another soft part of her he ached to explore. With only that need in mind, he plunged a hand beneath her skirt, finding her thigh. One searching caress upward, and he soon located what awaited between them.

The fabric of her skirt obscured his view. Through touch alone, he explored her with the tips of his fingers at first. Just one. Another.

Even through the thin panties she wore, he couldn't remember ever feeling something so soft. So delicate. Her heat was a furnace, scorching him from the outside before he even dared to stroke along a thatch of soft curls to tease the flesh beneath. He didn't know what to expect. Going off her holier than though speeches regarding daemons, he assumed she'd recoil from him—though she'd endured his touch before.

Last time, however, he'd been shocked to find she'd been slick with the faintest layer of moisture. Now, the material shielding her from him was already noticeably dampened. Soaked.

Gods above.

When she didn't resist, he eased a thumb between her and the material. Then, he cautiously slid that finger inside her, sucking in a breath at the warmth that greeted him. Her frigid exterior definitely didn't translate to that part of her body. She was molten, spasming in pleasure merely from his *touch*.

"Damn," he grated, withdrawing his lips from hers.

She wasn't quivering in fear. He extracted his fingers to be sure, watching them glisten in the lamplight. There was no mistaking her arousal. The smell tinged the air, so sweet he couldn't resist sampling a drop with his tongue.

And he was undone.

"Gods above, you taste like..."

Destruction—*his* if he didn't come to his senses and soon. He knew that. For thousands of years, he'd taught himself the risks of letting another woman get too close, let alone another witch.

None of that mattered.

One taste of her blinded him completely. Hungrily, he lowered his hand, sliding another finger inside of her. She tensed with a whine, but gradually her grip eased. So he gently added another finger, spreading them just enough to give a taste of fullness.

The witch groaned, and more moisture slicked her channel. Her head went back, her eyelids fluttering. When he began to stroke those invading digits, her hips arched against him, and he knew that she'd lied before.

She'd never experienced pleasure like this. Not from any man. Just him.

Her body reflected that lack. She was so tight. He groaned at the feel of her, unable to even imagine how she'd feel around his cock.

And, damn millennia of celibacy, he wanted to know. Needed to.

"Are you a virgin?" he asked, his voice hoarse. Hurting her was the furthest thing from his mind. He would take his time, no matter how much it pained him to bear her nearness for even a second longer. "Tell me if you are."

She stiffened, her eyes widening. "Get... Get off of me—"

"I will stop if you want me to." He didn't know why he felt compelled to tell her that. Strangely enough, the promise seemed to resonate within them both. Her eyes met his, swollen with alarm, and he felt a protectiveness unfurl swiftly, catching him off guard.

Even Liva never roused this feeling in him.

"You are used to people hurting you," he surmised from her reaction. Not sexually, perhaps, but in ways that made her flinch even when a daemon offered her a hint of mercy.

She wasn't just accustomed to pain. She didn't know how to react to the absence of it.

"I want you willing, witch," he added. "I won't force you."

"N-No!" She shook her head, too prideful to even accept that much. "As if I would ever want you," she croaked.

But he wanted her, and that was the terrifying part. A truth the animal in him couldn't deny, though the logical daemon lord wanted nothing more than to do so.

He wanted this woman in every way imaginable. The lust felt unnatural. Primal. Liva held appeal to him, but never with this raw intensity. In that small way, Miranda differed from her predecessor—and a pinch in his gut warned that it wasn't a good sign.

She made him too reckless. Too unstable. She made him want far more than he had any right to take.

"Go." He lurched to his feet, turning his back to her. "Now!"

He heard her scramble from the bed, her heartbeat unsteady, but he didn't dare turn to watch her leave. Only as her footsteps trailed into the hall did he realize that he'd driven her from the very haven he offered her in the first place.

The irony seemed fitting.

TWENTY-SEVEN

Miranda ran. She didn't stop until she was safely within the confines of Peony's storeroom, but even this space didn't feel far enough away from Atiernan.

She needed the distance only separate realms could ensure. Or different planets.

"Here already?" Peony called from the back of the room. "You could have slept some. I can tell from your eyes that you haven't."

"No," Miranda spat. "There isn't time to sleep."

She needed to break the tether drawing the creatures here, and end this.

Now.

Before Atiernan decided to sample far more than her blood.

But would she resist him? The question haunted her. She wanted to believe so. The daemon, with his slick words and obvious handsomeness, hadn't fooled her. She wouldn't break.

But she was still mortal at her core, and humans were susceptible to weakness. In terms of willpower and sheer muscle, Atiernan would always win.

So she would run.

"You look determined," Peony remarked as Miranda sank to her knees beside the cauldron. "Have you thought of a way to anchor your spell?"

"Better," Miranda admitted. "I discovered the source of your sentinel troubles. Part of it, anyway."

With a sigh, she told Peony everything. To her credit, the mage only looked partly shocked. Mainly, she seemed uneasy, as if Miranda had merely confirmed her worst fear.

"It lied to you," she said. "Atiernan and I are long-lived, but I told you it is not a common lifespan. And the cost we paid to attain such... I refuse to believe that creature has lived so long. It lied—"

"Why do you call him 'it'?" Miranda demanded, turning to find the mage watching her. "He has a name, *Marcus*. Because he is a hybrid, he isn't worthy of being referred to as a living person? Just a thing?"

Peony sighed, her eyes uncharacteristically gentle. "I know Liva. Any creature she had a hand in creating could have only come from the vilest evil."

"Some may say that about me," Miranda admitted with a cold laugh. "Evil. Vile. Abomination. I've heard it all before. I've endured years of people referring to me as 'it,' refusing to address me by name. You speak of Liva's evil, but ignorance and hate can fester as well. Those who called me monster were worse than what they accused me of being. I never had a choice!"

"I've offended you," Peony said softly. "You have every right to be angry. I apologize."

But that made it worse. Were she still in the coven, she would be scolded with a long list of her inherent sins. How was it that a group of daemons could show her more grace and mercy than the beings she'd spent her entire life believing were the superior race? How she used to long to be pure-blooded. To be without the taint of her father's race. To be worthy of her mother's love.

To exist without guilt.

She'd always comforted herself with the belief that as cruel as they were, the witches had raised her. Fed her. Clothed her. Daemons would have killed her at birth.

Or so her mother claimed.

First Atiernan, now Peony, offered her words of sympathy that no witch ever had. It didn't make sense. It felt…wrong. Her understanding of the world had always been the sole foundation she could trust—but now it sported cracks that grew with every second she spent in captivity.

"I need air," she spat, rising to her feet. Peony didn't follow her as she raced from the room.

Blindly, she ran, spotting few guards as she went. The manor was on alert still, but the danger from the breach had passed, meaning she met no resistance as she slipped out of a side door and into the crisp morning air.

The sky was a haunting shade of gray that heralded a storm, and a harsh wind nipped at her skin. She moved aimlessly, but stayed within the boundary of the inner walls. Any minute she expected Peony to come after her. Or even Atiernan himself.

Let him come. Then she could tell him the source of the spell and return to Hazel's Way.

She needed to go home.

Even if no one there wanted her back.

A wave of unexpected despair slammed into her, and she staggered, leaning against the bark of a nearby tree. Eyeing the sky, she indulged the pain for a second—just one. She let herself feel all the hurt and anguish and guilt. Then she banished it to the farthest reaches of her mind, where it belonged.

Enough crying.

It was time to go back and do the one thing she excelled at. She pulled herself upright and turned toward the house. Before she'd taken a step, a crack broke the quiet—as if a stick had snapped underfoot.

"Who's there?" she asked, scanning the nearby trees. No one came into view, but a tendril of unease ran down her spine. Someone was there, alright, watching from the shadows. "Atiernan?"

It was a wild guess, though something told her the daemon lord wouldn't spy on her from a hidden perch. No. He would stalk out to meet her boldly and observe her with the full knowledge that she watched.

And that she was helpless against him.

Whatever games the daemon wanted to play, she wouldn't humor him now.

"Hide if you want," she scoffed. "I'm going inside…"

A dark shape rushed toward her from her peripheral vision, though she couldn't turn in time to see them clearly. From far away, she heard a sickening thud, and everything turned black.

CHAPTER
TWENTY-EIGHT

Atiernan stayed away from her until he couldn't anymore. Reluctant footsteps carried him to Peony's storeroom, but as he rounded the doorway, he felt surprisingly...

Anxious.

Would the little witch pretend she hadn't been aroused by his fingers?

A part of him wanted her to. He would gladly refresh her memory, though he knew shyness wasn't what restrained her. Just pride.

She considered herself far too pure to be pleasured by a daemon, and he would take great enjoyment out of pleasuring her again.

And again.

With a low chuckle, he steeled himself to face her, already drunk on her scent. But when he finally entered the room, the witch was nowhere to be found.

"I was hoping you were Miranda," Peony said sadly once she spied him from her position in a far corner. "I spoke foolishly, and she ran off. Trust me to offend the one witch you've taken a liking to after several thousand years."

"What makes you think I've taken a liking to her?" Atiernan replied.

Peony threw her head back, cackling all the while. "Atiernan, if I hadn't learned by now how to tell what you're thinking, I wouldn't have made good use of the past millennia, now would I?"

"And if I have?"

Peony sighed, her expression surprisingly thoughtful. He would have thought she'd be hissing at the thought of him taking another witch as a lover. "Then I would warn you to be careful, Atiernan. Though, I also know that I wouldn't have to tell you that. If anyone knows the danger of a cunning witch, it is you."

"But you like her as well," he pointed out. "Enough to speak to her cordially anyway."

Peony shrugged. "I like her grit. Few of her kind could go toe to toe with a sentinel and live to tell the tale."

"When she returns, send her to me," Atiernan said. "There is much I need to discuss with the witch."

"I will. That being said, be careful, Atiernan. You are strong, but no one is infallible."

Her words echoed in his skull as he left the room, finding his way into the great hall. Once there, reality returned with a vengeance—Miranda was far from the only concern he had to deal with. There was repairing the outer wall for one. Then arranging the guard on the captive sentinel and marshaling his men to perform nightly patrols. He threw himself into the busywork, letting the monotony wash every trace of the witch from his brain.

But, stubbornly, Miranda remained.

He couldn't get her taste off his tongue, or her face from his mind. He needed to see her, but as the hours stretched on, she eluded him. Two more trips to Peony's storeroom revealed no sign of her. He even checked the room he'd assigned her.

When it too turned up empty, his confusion turned to anger.

So the bitch thought to evade him in his own damn manor? He would find her, and when he did…

He'd take out his frustration on that beautiful body. Inch by inch. His mouth watered at the prospect, and he continued his search in earnest.

Rather than hunches, he relied on his senses, tracking her scent again near the storeroom, but beyond it. Outside into the courtyard he'd found her in before. Only she wasn't there. Her scent grew strongest near a grove of trees and then faded.

As if she'd vanished into midair.

Because, of course, she had. With her magic, he had no real way of restraining her, either.

"My lord!" Benjamin rushed to him from the direction of the perimeter. "You should see this," he said grimly.

Atiernan followed him to the outer wall. There, sliced into the stone itself, was a crack. One thin enough for a determined sentinel to enter via.

Or a witch to exit from.

"This was made with magic," the man explained. "Another breach. If it wasn't discovered in time…"

The sentinels would have gotten inside the inner courtyard, where the youngest of the pack played.

"Who discovered it?" Atiernan asked.

"One of the men," Benjamin said. "But that isn't all. They found the witch in the process of using her magic. Thankfully, they were able to restrain her."

"Miranda…" A growl broke from his throat as he pictured her, gleefully attempting to lure another sentinel inside. "Where is she now?"

"The one place her magic has no power," Benjamin said softly. "You remember it?"

He did, and ironically it wasn't long ago that he taunted Miranda with that very prison.

The crypt.

CHAPTER
TWENTY-NINE

It was dark.

Dark.

Black.

The air felt so still it was suffocating, the silence broken only by her own panting breaths.

Don't panic. She chanted that mantra over and over. *Don't panic. Never panic.* As her thoughts formed some semblance of coherence again, she exhaled raggedly. Then she tracked the time.

It was the only way to keep her sanity while in the dark—logically track each passing second. She couldn't stay in here forever. Even daemons wouldn't leave her here to rot.

One minute. Two…

An eternity.

The more she became aware of her surroundings, the more uneasy she felt. This wasn't her cell, but somewhere enclosed. Small. Cramped. There wasn't enough room to sit up. With every attempt, her hands brushed the immovable walls. She couldn't stand. Move.

Breathe!

"Please..." Her voice broke, shrill to her own ears. "Please, let me out. Hello?"

No one answered.

"Please!"

Nothing.

Because no one was there, of course. Once armed with her greatest fear, Atiernan had rushed to exploit it. They left her here to die. They buried her alive. She was dying...

Save yourself.

No. She resisted the thought mentally at first. Then shouted it. Screamed.

"No!"

No, she wouldn't. She couldn't.

Save yourself, Miranda.

This place wasn't the dungeon, or even the cellar she was used to. It was too small. *A tomb,* a part of her whispered. Atiernan had taunted her with that very prison, after all. There was no escape from it. She would die here otherwise. Die alone in the dark, forgotten.

Save yourself!

Her forearm brushed her lips, and she shivered as she felt the wounds Atiernan left behind. Only now could she admit it—his bite hadn't hurt, and that puzzled her still.

Because when her own teeth bit into her flesh…

It hurt like hell. Her screams deafened her as the taste of blood flooded her mouth. This magic required more than even Atiernan took.

Rivulets of blood until she felt as though she were drowning in it. Choking.

Forming the spell itself required no thought or input. No knowledge or skill. Just primal, pathetic instinct.

A single, overriding need.

In this moment? She needed out. Gods, she needed out now! She needed…

Air! She breathed in so deeply that she coughed. No longer was she trapped in a small space but somewhere bright. So bright her eyes stung as she peeled them open. Was that sunlight? She craned her neck, expecting to find Atiernan's fortress, not brick.

She barely noted the modern trappings of this structure—electrical wires and the telltale bustle of nearby traffic—when the icy feel of metal bit into her throat.

"What the hell are you doing here?" a cold voice snarled against her ear.

Her first instinct was to scream. Then she realized…

That voice was familiar.

"Answer me, daemon," the figure demanded, but the cadence of his voice triggered a memory. He couldn't be... "Speak! Or so help me, I'll—"

"M-Marcus?"

It seemed unlikely, but she knew in her soul the figure wasn't Atiernan. This voice was softer, and as for where they were…

It wasn't the daemon's fortress by any stretch of the imagination. The sun shone brighter, with regular buildings instead of trees. The architecture was modern as well. Almost like the small town on the outskirts of the forest where her coven dwelled. Somewhere far beyond the daemon realm, in any case.

"You are the hybrid witch." The man holding her spun her to face him.

Her first thought was that she'd been wrong. Atiernan faced her after all. They even wore the same expression when openly suspicious. Eyes narrowed, lips pursed, and an eyebrow raised. Then she noted the man's black hair instead of blood red. His eyes were dark too, and his physical build slightly more gracile.

"How did you find me?" he asked. His voice was decidedly softer, not that she took much comfort in that.

How ironic that she had escaped one monster only to run into another.

Would he imprison her too?

"You used blood magic." The man's gaze was on her forearm. "Shit—"

Dazed, Miranda looked down to find that she was bleeding, dripping scarlet liquid onto the concrete at her feet. She hated how her blood looked like this. Redder than a normal witch's. Deeper. As if even her very cells had no choice but to proclaim her otherness to the world.

With every drop, the truth spilled out—she was tainted. Filthy. Wrong.

"Did you lead him to me?" Marcus demanded, sounding miles away. "Answer me!"

He reached for her, and Miranda reacted purely on instinct. She was the little girl forced to do her mother's bidding. Weak. Pathetic.

She screamed.

Then she wailed in a way she hadn't in years.

As if her heart had exploded and bled from her eyes in the form of tears.

Sobs she feared would never end.

THIRTY

Atiernan seethed. When he got his hands around her throat, he was going to kill the wench. Then toss her body onto the pyre along with the creature he should have killed rather than let her keep in his dungeon like a pet.

That had been her plan all along—to use the creature to lure in more.

And he'd obeyed like some love-struck puppy.

Damn her.

Still, as he followed Benjamin into the dungeon, he couldn't hear her mocking voice echoing off the walls. Or smell her scent. Just something sharper. Like…

"Where is she?" he demanded.

"I had no choice, my lord," Benjamin said, rounding a section of the manor that served as a crypt. "This was the only place that could hold a witch."

Atiernan frowned, only spying marble coffins that held the ashes of daemons long since departed. "What do you..."

He homed in on one vessel, in particular, the only one with a disturbed layer of dust.

"You locked her inside a tomb."

On the one hand, it was a clever way to hold an unbound witch at risk of using her magic to wreak havoc. On the other...

They locked me in until I obeyed...

"Open it!" He surged forward and gripped one end of the massive lid. "Now!"

Benjamin rushed to obey, grabbing the stone slab's other side. It had been cracked to let in just enough air for her to breathe, but the darkness would be impenetrable. If she dreaded the dungeon, he couldn't imagine how she'd feel in such an enclosed space.

Together, he and Ben wrenched off the lid, letting it fall with a deafening thud.

But the space within was empty.

"Where is she?"

Benjamin gaped. "I... I swear she was here, my lord."

Atiernan whirled on him, raising a fist.

Then he smelled it. That sharp, sweet scent magnified tenfold. When he inspected the coffin again, it was still empty, save for a substance he hadn't noticed before, streaked along both sides.

Blood. Miranda's blood.

It was fresh, far too much to be from her healing sentinel marks.

"You harmed her?" He saw red as he turned to Benjamin. The other man didn't have the chance to speak before he had his hands around his throat. "You dared to harm her?"

"N-No, my lord! I—"

"Atiernan."

He turned to discover Peony standing at the mouth of the room. Was he surprised to find her always one step ahead? No.

Her stern frown, however, caught him off guard. His initial fear was that something had happened to Beth, but no. Peony only reserved that expression for him, and the last time she'd worn it had been the day another witch tried to have him killed.

Perhaps, speaking first was his attempt to stall the inevitable, but he found his lips parting regardless. "Miranda is gone—"

"I heard," the mage said grimly. "She might have just returned to her coven—"

"Or she was an agent of Liva all along, and she could be plotting with her as we speak," Atiernan interjected. Did he truly believe that? He didn't know.

"Yes," Peony agreed with a sigh. "Though, either way, we won't have to worry about her betrayal for long. But there is something you should know about her."

He released Benjamin and gripped the edge of the tomb. Damn. This was nothing like what happened with Liva. He'd never heard her so grave. He'd never felt this…uneasy.

You won't have to worry for long…

Why was that?

"Speak!" he demanded.

"I will tell you this alone," Peony said, prompting Benjamin to leave. "But I will warn you now that you won't like it. There is one positive, however. If she has left the confines of the manor, she'll be dead before tomorrow night."

"But that isn't what has you worried," Atiernan surmised. "Tell me."

"To put it bluntly—she has the power to destroy us all, Atiernan," Peony said with a sad shrug. "I won't deny it, and I believed her trustworthy, but we can't take the risk if she isn't. If she is an agent of Liva, our only hope is to leave before they send a horde of monsters to tear us to pieces. Now. There isn't even time to scout out a new territory. We must flee."

The sheer desperation of that statement—paired with Peony's usual calm demeanor—drove the point home like a hammer on a nail.

He had failed. By trusting Miranda even a fraction, he had opened up his people to untold pain and destruction.

Again.

For the second time, a witch had fooled him, and his people would suffer in return.

Strangely, anger wasn't what he felt surging through his veins, building in intensity with every fierce beat of his heart.

Just a vicious, unending bloodlust.

"Atiernan?" Peony prodded. "Did you hear what I said?"

"Do what you think is necessary," he replied in a voice he didn't recognize. "Leave the witch to me. An agent of Liva or not, I will find her… And when I do, I will kill her."

~ Atiernan and Miranda's story continues in Daemon's Kiss ~

A WORD FROM THE AUTHOR

Hey there!

Thank you so much for reading! If you enjoyed the story, please leave a review and recommend the book to any friend you think would love this twisted world. You'd have my eternal gratitude. Even a short sentence goes a long way!

Then, come join the rest of us dark romance lovers in my Facebook Group where you can get snippets, sneak peeks of upcoming books and even help vote on aspects of future novels.

Come to the dark side:
https://www.facebook.com/groups/lanasbeautifulmonsters/

WANT MORE STUFF TO READ?
Join my newsletter and get a **free book**! Plus, you get to stay updated with any new releases, random giveaways and exclusive sneak peeks!
https://www.lanaskybooks.com/newsletter

Other Novels: https://lanaskybooks.com/

FREE BOOK - JOIN MY NEWSLETTER

DARK, TWISTED ROMANCE

Join my newsletter and get a **free book**! Plus, you get to stay updated with any new releases, random giveaways and exclusive sneak peeks!

https://www.lanaskybooks.com/newsletter

ABOUT THE AUTHOR

Lana Sky is a reclusive writer in the United States who spends most of her time daydreaming about complex male characters and parenting her Cockapoo Joey. She writes dark, twisted romance across several genres. Her titles include everything from mafia romance to vampires.

facebook.com/AuthorLanaSky

twitter.com/lanasky101

amazon.com/author/lanasky

pinterest.com/lanasky101

goodreads.com/lanasky

instagram.com/lanasky101

bookbub.com/authors/lana-sky

tiktok.com/@author_lana_sky

ALSO BY LANA SKY

For more titles by Lana Sky, please visit:

https://www.lanaskybooks.com